I0619540

OUTCROSSING

MYSTERIOUS CHARM: BOOK 1

CELIA LAKE

CELIA LAKE

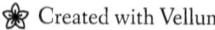

ALSO BY CELIA LAKE

The Mysterious Charm Series
Outcrossing
Goblin Fruit
Magician's Hoard
War
In The Cards
On The Bias
Seven Sisters

The Mysterious Powers Series
Carry On
The Fossil Door
Eclipse

Charms of Albion
Pastiche

Learn more about the world of Albion and future books at my website, celialake.com.

Sign up for my newsletter to be the first to hear about future books and learn about fascinating bits of research. Happy reading!

ABOUT OUTCROSSING

Having magic in your blood doesn't make you happy.

Rufus lost his brothers to the Great War and his parents to the Naples Scourge. He's on the verge of losing his New Forest cottage, his ponies, and any chance of a future. Everyone knows his magic is powerful, but no one trusts him, not anymore. When he saves Ferry's charge from a cranky pony on market day, she offers the first kind words he's heard in months.

Ferry became a governess in rural England to escape an arranged marriage. Six months later, she's (mostly) figured out how to manage her charges and begun to explore the nearby village and the forest around it. Rufus is everything her family would hate, but he loves and understands the New Forest in a way that enchants her. She'll gladly learn anything he's willing to teach.

When a smuggler needs his raw power to handle a rare shipment, Rufus can't resist the chance to make enough money to change his life forever. He has hope for the first time in years until the curiosity of the local lord and a completely inadequate magical education threaten the only home he's ever known and any possible future with Ferry.

Outcrossing is a standalone romance of 60,000 words with a happy ending (no cliffhangers). The Mysterious Charm series explores the magical community of the British Isles in the 1920s and can be read in any order.

Come to England's New Forest in 1922 and enjoy *Outcrossing*'s ponies, smugglers, and charm!

ONE

Rufus missed enjoying market days. When he'd been small, when things had been different, he'd always looked forward to them. A chance to spend a coin or two on something sweet, or to get a bruised apple from a stall after helping for a few minutes. He found it peaceful, watching the New Forest ponies wander in and through, the way people made space for them, the way the ponies were with each other.

These days, it was more complicated. He had to come to market, it was the best place to look for work, but he felt sure people were judging him every time he turned around.

It wasn't just him thinking so. He heard the questions here and there. Why was he here when their sons and brothers and fathers weren't? Was he going to get drunk and be difficult again? Why hadn't he gone and found steady work somewhere else?

Once, he'd thought people would understand how he couldn't leave, but also how staying felt like stone piled on stone, pinning him down and fencing him in. Now he was sure he'd not get another chance. Not enough of one.

He'd already walked down one side of the market street, glancing at stalls full of things he couldn't begin to afford. He lingered to watch one of the stalls demonstrate a hovering toy to a pair of boys. He remembered what it was like to press up against the table, watch the charms tumble a toy or spin it. The tisane stall drew him with the blends that soothed pain or eased dreams. She never had enough in stock these days, and the ingredients were dear as it was. Certainly beyond his meagre coins.

He ran his hands through his hair as he came to the high part of the road, turning around to look out at the stalls, trying to figure out where to try next. Peters sometimes had work hauling. Back-breaking work without the magic he hadn't learned, but he was decent enough, paid fairly. Talbot had said he might have something this week or maybe next, helping one of the carpenters. Mason was a brute to work for, but Rufus couldn't be picky. Not anymore. Nothing steady, even with Peters. Maybe enough to get him to the next week. Maybe.

The shift in the crowd caught his attention. It was like watching the ponies in a herd, the way people moved aside or closer, depending. In the midst of the eddy of people, there was a woman, a bit older than Rufus. Her dark blonde hair was coming loose from the bun at the back of her neck. He thought he'd seen her once or twice last autumn, before the weather turned, but she wasn't from the village.

She was trying to catch up to a boy with shining golden hair. Posher than she was, by the clothing. Hers was pleasant, a deep green dress and coat of what his mother would have said was a sensible sort of wool, but the boy was in nicer clothes. He danced across the main road, ducking and spinning between people.

"Caelus, come back here. Or there'll be no story with supper."

"You're not Nanny. You don't get to decide about stories!" The boy twisted around to stick out his tongue, waggle his fingers in his ears. There was a girl, too, picking her way more cautiously in the woman's wake, though held firmly by one hand.

"Caelus, come...oh, Merlin's sake..." And then the woman was fumbling in her shopping basket, a green stone on her pendant flashing in the sunlight. She brought something out, something that fit in her cupped palm, like a smooth flat river stone.

There was that moment Rufus could never look away from, the twist he could feel in the world, but not do deliberately. The boy stopped dead, caught by some magic from the stone. There were ponies milling about just behind the boy. Then Rufus heard the squeal of two mares gearing up to figure out who was dominant and who would go away with her tail pinned and ears back. One, the grey, was far too close to the boy, quite out of sorts, and in perfect kicking range.

Rufus was moving before he thought about it, feeling the warmth swell out inside him. He called out "Stand!" to the ponies as he swept the boy up in his arms. The boy squawked, but he couldn't wriggle. Whatever she'd got him with, it was too specific a magic.

Rufus crossed the street, trying to ignore the tsks and scandalized comments, and then carefully deposited the boy on his feet in front of his - no, not a nanny. Something else. He rubbed a hand - a grubby hand, he realised - across his face, and then offered a weak "Ma'am."

Not at all sure what to call her. He looked back at the ponies and made the little trilling sound his brother had taught him, the one that encouraged them to go back to their grazing.

When he turned to the woman again, she was bending down to peer at her charge, before she murmured a word and the charm relaxed. The boy tried to pull away, but she had a good hold of his wrist now, and the girl's hand in her other. Which at least meant she wasn't going to be shaking Rufus's dirty hand.

She looked him up and down, but unlike the tittering gossip he could still hear behind him, it didn't seem judgemental. Rather, she looked almost curious. Maybe he was imagining that.

She shifted, resettling her grip on the children. "Caelus, that was dangerous. You might have got hurt. Sir, thank you for your quick action."

Sir? There was no sir here. "Ma'am?" he said after a moment.

She nodded at him. "Thank you for that. I'm sure Caelus didn't realise at all what he was doing. I'm not used to the ponies among people like this yet, I'm not from the Forest."

He blinked again. And again. He was sure he must look daft. "Um. Not a sir, ma'am. A pleasure, ma'am. Easier that he couldn't wriggle, ma'am. That's quite a charm."

This made her break out in a warm smile. "I have a spinster aunt makes all manner of handy things. When she found out I would be a governess, she packed up a grand little box. Makes someone go quite still. They can overbalance, but it's a big help with a rascal like Caelus here." She was fond of her charge by the tone in her voice.

He blinked again, then ventured a "Don't know much about formal magic, ma'am, never had much schooling. Not like you." He gestured at the pendant. He'd heard about them, seen a couple up close. That setting and stone meant she'd gone to Schola.

Others could read what the colour meant, the details of the decoration. He couldn't. He just knew she was far better trained than he was, in ways he had no idea how to describe.

He realised with a start there'd been a long silence, then managed "I know more about the sort things you pick up living in the Forest."

This got her lighting up. "Oh, have you seen the wandermists? Do you know where they are? People keep telling me that they're incredible."

He coughed. "They're, um. Not predictable, ma'am." Decidedly not. He'd heard some people thought them related to dragons, and some to hummingbirds, and some to something else entirely. They were cat-sized, and as far as anyone could tell, made up of clouds of mist. They looked like a winged dragon that hovered upright then darted off to some other food or - well, whatever wander-mists did. No one was clear on much about them except their existence.

She beamed, and "Oh, that's what I heard. That thing about how they find blue flowers on the new moon, is that true, do you think? I read Fitzrandolph's *Bestiary* and Algernon Smythe-Clive's *Albion's Fair Creatures*, but they disagree about the habitat, of course - Fitzrandolph thinks they live in swamps, and well...."

Her voice trailed off as she realised someone else was trying to get her attention. It was one of the older matrons, peering down her nose and over rimmed glasses. "Ferry Wright, I do declare. Bring those children with you. We simply must catch up." Clipped voice, the accent of one of the women of the Forest villages. A woman who aspired to better things than a cottage in the woods and a little herd of ponies and sheep and pigs and chickens.

Ferry ducked her head and said, "Sorry, um. Mrs Wain is really quite, um. I wouldn't want to upset her. She knows several of my aunts. Thank you again. I'm Ferry Wright. Sorry, meant to say."

He barely had time to say "Rufus Pride."

The moment he'd said that, the disapproving older woman was tugging her off, the children along with her, to one of the village tea houses. Mrs Wain would clearly be talking Miss Wright's ear off about the unsuitability of people like Rufus. He shook his head, and then again, to clear it. Then he set off to talk to people who might give him a bit of work. He did his best to ignore the gossip that continued around him, which got quiet whenever he got close enough he might hear.

TWO

TRUE EYEWORTH

T he scolding began almost immediately. "Now, Feronia, Ferry, dear, I know you're not used to our little Forest communities yet, but you must realise that it will do you no good to stand in the street talking with every working man you come across, or any of them, for that matter. And especially not that one." Her tone was very disapproving. "What in magic's green blessings were you thinking, dear?"

Ferry ducked her chin and murmured. "Beg pardon, Mrs Wain. He'd - well, Caelus had got out of my hand, and far too close to a pony that was upset."

"Oh, pish posh, Ferry, you silly dear, I know you're not used to living so near the Forest, but the ponies are really the sweetest things, all goodness and beauty, don't you think? Gentle as a lamb, every single one of them."

Ferry barely managed to avoid rolling her eyes at this. She'd seen ponies with her own eyes who got in fights. She wasn't sure why they did, but she'd seen them, she wanted to learn more about why. The mares had such spirit, not like most of the women she knew. Or the woman she was, for that matter.

And she'd seen the ears go back, and the necks arching, and that curious tension in the spine and the haunches. If that was the word. She hadn't been able to take Magical Fauna at school. It wasn't considered proper for a girl from a family like hers.

She rode, of course, that was expected. But only well-trained docile mounts who didn't kick or buck or bite, prepared by a groom and brought out to the stableyard. She was never even allowed to see them at rest except from a distance, well on the other side of a sturdy fence. All the old traditions, that she must keep, whether she wanted to or not.

And then there was the young man, Rufus. She'd liked the look of him. He seemed different than the people she knew, unpolished, more real. His dark red hair had been long enough to move in the wind, not pinned back into submission or cut so short it stayed in place. She also liked how he'd seen a problem and fixed it. He'd been kind without reason. It made her look past the fact his clothes needed mending, and his shoes were muddy and most of him needed a bath.

Mrs Wain was going on and on, while Ferry was distracted, and then there was a sudden silence Ferry was clearly supposed to fill, and Ferry wasn't.

"Pardon, ma'am. I'm sorry, I couldn't quite hear that." There was, at least, a conveniently placed older witch nearby, somewhat deaf, who would insist on bellowing when she wanted to say something.

Mrs Wain tsked at her. "You really must pay attention, Ferry, dear, it's not nice to ask someone to repeat them-selves. Quite destroys the elegant flow of conversation you want to create, now that is your role as a companion in conversation, to help encourage the conversation, not to turn it to your own interests. No one wants to hear about those, dear, it's not all appropriate for you to have interests of your own."

Ferry managed not to blow hair out of her face, but she took a breath, waited for a pause in the scolding disguised with sugar, and then said "I would appreciate your help, Mrs Wain, in what I could do better next time to manage Caelus in a crowd. He's so good at home, but of course, there are so many things to see at market day."

Ferry had not meant to be a governess, after all, but it was a suitable sort of occupation for a young woman from a good family who was refusing to get married. Not that she'd have known what to tell anyone if they'd asked what she wanted, as she wasn't sure herself. She'd shown no strong particular talent at school in anything she'd been permitted to do coursework in, and no idea if the things she had been forbidden might go any better.

In the quiet of her room at night, she admitted to herself she wanted something different than running a large house, or having formal parties, or worrying about the clothes she was wearing. Even if she was not at all sure how to deal with teaching children, that was something meaningful and practical. And it was vastly better than marriage to a man near three times her age she'd met twice and immediately disliked.

Her question at least got Mrs Wain off on a more agreeable topic, even if it did take her five minutes to suggest that keeping hold of his hand was probably the only viable solution. Or perhaps a short leash attached to a harness. She finally could venture a "Mrs Wain, I do - I know it's not at all proper, but the man I was speaking to. So I know how to avoid him, or people like him, what should I know?"

This got her a lengthy but informative lecture. Rufus Pride was the youngest of four brothers, the other three all killed in the War, like Mrs Wain's eldest. He'd somehow come back without a scratch on him, which Mrs Wain thought entirely improper, and not long after that, his parents had both died in the Naples Scourge. Then, he'd clearly not followed anyone's idea of a proper life for a survivor.

"Oh, people tried to help him out, for memory of his family. His father, quite a steady worker, and his mother had a really deft hand with a needle, a lot of little tricks to make sure what she made or mended stayed that way. And his eldest brother, Jasper, he was apprenticing with the Alfreds, and they've always had quite a way with horses, it was quite the coup that they took Jasper on."

Mrs Wain, however, was very dismissive of Rufus, though it took listening to what she wasn't saying for Ferry to put some of it together. He'd not been visibly grateful in the proper ways for his outrageously good fortune and had turned to drink and scrabbling to get by in rough jobs with unsavoury types. Mrs Wain finished up with a "And I've heard tell he even speaks to … to the Gentleman of the Night." The smugglers.

Mrs Wain clearly wanted some response, and Ferry murmured "Oh, my. I'm so glad you were willing to tell me more, Mrs Wain. It's good I can rely on you to tell me what I need to know about people here." And then she cleared her throat and a "I'm so sorry, but I did promise Nanny Ogden that I'd pick up a few things for her, and I really don't want to disappoint her, you know how she gets when she doesn't have embroidery silks, and she's out of at least three colours."

This got "Oh, and are you working on a project, dear,

you really ought, it's entirely a proper occupation for a young woman, and so useful." To which Ferry had to demur, that she loved the colours, but she just didn't seem to be that skilled with it. What she didn't say was that every time she tried, it was technically competent, but somehow entirely flat and lifeless and the eye slid past it quickly. She thought this was not a useful trait in a decorative object at all, but explaining that never went well.

Nanny Ogden was, as usual, an excellent excuse, and it was only another couple of minutes before she was ducking out of the teahouse, after cleaning the crumbs of sugar off the faces of her charges. "Right, you both. Let's get the embroidery floss, and then you can each pick out a book."

Bribery never hurt. She was lucky that her charges could be bribed with storybooks, which were the kind of thing their parents would never think to get them. Their ever-travelling neglectful parents liked the idea of children rather a lot more than the reality, and brought home things that were vastly inappropriate.

She steered them to the embroidery silk, chose the colours Nanny wanted, and then it was time to climb the worn steps of the shop two down, and push the door of the bookshop open.

"Afternoon, Pross!" Her friend Proserpina was settled at the desk by the door, her usual place.

It had clearly not been as busy a day as she might have hoped, but the older woman smiled and said "Ferry, I was hoping you'd be in. I've a book set aside for you. Cardea, sweetheart, there's a new series I discovered you might like, and Caelus, I think you're a young man who wants a book about dragons, and there's a gorgeous new one come in."

"Does it do anything?" Caelus was cheerful.

"It's a book. It tells you things!" Proserpina's usual

answer made him grin. "It also has enchanted illustrations that show different parts of a dragon's body moving, and even some illusions of them. Cammie's back in the storeroom if you want to ask her to show you where it is." The two scampered off to the back with Pross' daughter.

Pross murmured "A little dear, but within the book budget, if perhaps not your formal curriculum."

Ferry laughed. "Well, if I kept to that, it'd be dry literature from the best magical authors and only the best magical authors, and we'd all be asleep by half ten in the morning with boredom."

Pross shook her head. "And their parents, still travelling?"

Ferry nodded. "No idea when they'll be home. The last letter we had was a fortnight ago, they were leaving Egypt and going toward somewhere cooler for the summer months. I thought they might return here before setting off again, but I gather not." She looked after her charges, for a moment. "It seems a poor way to raise children."

Pross shook her head. "Not the way I raise Cammie, not all. Or that her father would if he were still here." She blew her hair out of her face. "How's the market? It's been too quiet in here."

Ferry shook her head. "Busy. People liking being out on the streets, a pleasant day, maybe? Caelus almost got in more trouble than I want to think about - you know how he gets away from me in the crowd, sometimes? He got far too near a couple of the ponies and nearly got kicked, I got the charm out, but a man snatched him up and brought him back, out of harm's way. I got scolded about it. Mrs Wain, of course."

Pross groaned. "Oh, she's on you again? Do you think your aunt's been writing to her?"

Ferry shook her head. "She actually didn't say? I got a good quarter hour about what I should be doing differently. And then I did get her to tell me about the man - a forester, I guess. Rufus Pride? Around my age, dark red hair, bit taller than me, broad shoulders, sort of scruffy?" The last part was a bit tentative, even if it was true.

Pross made a face. "Oh, that's a sad story. Last of his family, though of course he's loosely related to a good number of the Forest folk. Had a rough time of it since he came home from the War, no money, only the family cottage, and even keeping that's a near thing, no one thinks he'll pay the tithe this year. They turned their hand to a variety of work, and I gather he's not bad with horses, but there's not much work there after the War. Not for someone without a reason to be chosen for it."

Ferry asked, carefully "Same sort of worries as you, that way, then?" and Pross nodded. Ferry took a breath, then changed the subject. "Anyway, for all Mrs Wain thought he was apparently below consideration, I thought he was quite polite. Though he called me ma'am a lot, and it's not like I'm older than he is. Or not by much?"

Pross snorted. "No, but you're posh. You carry yourself like posh, you know that."

Ferry made a face. "Not that it's actually good for much as it turns out."

"Have you heard from your parents? Or that great-aunt?"

Ferry shook her head. "Mother and Father are still upset I wouldn't even consider Joachim Elder, and Great-Aunt Aurelia is furious about that. Despite him being sixty." She made a face. "And him being a boring old drone."

Pross tapped her fingers on the desk, standing to

rummage for something. "And other things. So you're still in exile for a bit more. Good for me, anyway. Come on, I'll show you that book I think you'll like. We can give the children a bit of time to play. Speaking of, can I bring Cammie up to you on Tuesday? I have a few meetings I'd rather not have her around for."

Ferry nodded, and they went off to examine books and keep an eye on the various children.

THREE

TRUE EYEWORTH

F ive days later, Rufus couldn't stop thinking about her. It was Friday, and he was at loose ends. The bits of work he'd picked up had tapered off. His snares had been empty this morning. He had enough for cheap bread and maybe a bit of cheese until Monday, but not much more. No idea what he'd do then. He'd lost the last of the chickens to a fox, a month back, so there wasn't even the promise of eggs.

He walked down the path in the forest, kicking a stone here or there out of his way, glancing up periodically to see the deer in the distance bob and shift. Everything felt stuck. Bogged down in mud, and nothing he could do would begin to firm it up. Nothing he could do would ever be anything more than this endless round of never being good enough, of people stepping away from him, muttering about him, resenting him.

It had been different in the War. The War had been horrible, every bit of it, from training to the trenches. He'd hated the shouting and the strictness, how any little misstep was a wave drowning him. He had done his duty, more than done his duty. He had to shake himself before the memories of the trench collapse got too much and forced him to his knees in the middle of the road, and he tried to think of something else, anything else.

Which brought him right back to Miss Wright.

It had been a while since anyone had been interested in anything he had to say. Peters and Talbot and Mason gave him work, and they weren't cruel - well, mostly. But they weren't friendly, they didn't want conversation. Just his hands and his back and all his labour for not much in the way of coin.

She wasn't from the Forest. He was sure of that. He knew most of the people around his age. Well, he'd known them, the ones who were dead now. And the sisters, some were married, some were gone to jobs, to fill in for the men who weren't here. Taking on jobs below stairs in posh households, learning the magics of cleaning silverware and silks. The unmarried women were kept close at home, well away from the likes of him.

It wasn't any better in the common villages. He was known in a few of them, Peters had put him on to a couple of jobs moving wood. But they found him even more suspicious and - just wrong, one of the wives had called him. "Nothing natural about a man coming out of the War, not a scratch on him." He couldn't explain it, he barely knew why it was. Or why him, and not his brothers.

Here he was going down the wrong road in his head again. Thinking about his brothers never ended well at all.

Miss Wright, she wasn't from here. But she was clearly in charge of the children. He thought he remembered seeing the two of them when they were younger, out with an older grey-haired woman who walked with a cane, back when he was home on leave before shipping out to France. The last time he'd seen his parents.

He'd been distracted, that whole trip, feeling like there wasn't enough time to drink it all in, in case he didn't come back, but they'd gone into town, for his Da to take him to the pub, one last drink. He thought he'd seen the woman and the children then, some special treat.

He was deep in such melancholy thoughts, plodding along the track from Fritham toward home, when he almost ran into a cart with a black cob mare, stuck in a bit of mud. There was a man there, one he didn't know. The cart was open-topped, loaded with wooden shipping boxes and a couple of trunks. There was nothing that looked too heavy, the way the mare was warm but not covered in sweat, but more than someone could shift on their own.

"Pardon, are you stuck? Can I help you?" And then he took in the cart, the man's tweeds, and there was an automatic, reflexive, "Sir?"

The sandy-haired man stood up, with a bit of a grunt. "She's well and truly stuck." Posh accent, though with something a bit odd about it, that clipped drawl.

Rufus considered, then said "Glad to see if I can help get her free? We're a fair bit from any village, sir."

The pony hitched to the cart nickered, and the man patted her gently on the shoulder. "There's a girl, Gossip, settle a little."

The name startled Rufus. "Gossip, sir?"

The man grinned suddenly. "Always talking with her neighbours in the stable. If you can find a way to shift it, I'd be obliged. Too much in the back to carry, and some might spoil if it was left."

Rufus almost asked, and then shook his head. "Let me look, sir. I have a strong back, maybe together we can manage." He walked around the cart, picked up a stick from the side of the road, prodded at the ground by the wheels.

"Sir, I think." He paused, then he caught the ring on the man's hand, this one with a shimmering white stone. He swallowed, then there's a "Sir, if you're capable, there might be a thing. I don't know how, but I know the - physical things that might help?" He kept his wording so careful. Out here, this might be someone with the magic, or someone not. The rules of the Silence were absolute, for all the Forest held both kinds of people.

The man got suddenly curious. "You do, now?" And then a, "Magic folk, yourself?"

Rufus nodded. "Sir," he said in agreement, and then he had to clarify. "Never had no formal training, sir. Apprenticed, sir, as the War started. He had to go fight early. Years before I was old enough." He felt himself get quieter at the end, for what might have been different. "Burleigh, if you know the name."

His master, his would-have-been master, who'd told him he had potential, who'd listened, who'd believed he could make something of himself beside rough labour and farmwork and secret words muttered in the ears of horses. Who never came back, buried far away in France where he couldn't even go yell at the grave like he did with his parents.

"Heard well of him." And then he tapped his fingers on the carriage. "You'd be... one of the Pride boys. You have the face for it. Rud... No, Rufus, wasn't it? A good Forest name." For the dead king. And it did go with his red hair.

Rufus ducked his chin. "Sir."

The man nodded. "Geoffrey Carillon. Heir to Ytene, these days, the estate. Well, Lord of it, actually." He made a face and gestured north and west. "Newly back here. Forgot about the mud lasting as long as it does in the shade."

Rufus was startled. Not many posh folk would put it that way. Either the introduction or noticing the mud was lingering. "Sir, Lord Carillon." he said again, so careful now before he ventured a, "The thing it wants is something solid to push against. Without magic, I'd go find a board, four of them, wedge under the wheels, so you could get traction. But we're a good two mile from somewhere'd have good boards cut, and it's near three already." Half an hour or so back to Ytene, if they could get the cart free.

"And we don't want to be alone in this stretch of wood at night, no. I've heard the tales. Opportunist Gentlemen of the Night. And then there are wandermists, and botolons, and ginsies. I've heard that ginsies aren't nearly so bad as the stories say, I'd rather not discover it for myself with no preparation." Seeing as half the people who touched them died within a day, no.

Rufus nodded. "So, sir," he prompted. "Do you know anything that might help? Not to make all the ground solid - that's the thing I know how to do, but if I do it now, the wheels will stay stuck. We just want the space below where you want them to go. I'm afraid I'm not good at doing it in a small enough space."

Lord Carillon made a face and then nodded. "Think so. Actually, moment." He paused, and went around the back of the cart, opening up a chest. "Bought a book has - something..." He thumbed through it, carefully, like the pages were fragile, but not slowly, before he peered at it, and casually cast a ball of light to hover at his shoulder with a snap of his fingers to read it better in the shadows of the trees. "Ah, I thought there was something. Yes, now I've got an idea." He rummaged in his long cloak for a moment and brought out a small wand.

Not everyone used them. Not even most people. They weren't essential for magic. Master Burleigh had said they were rather like an automobile. Undeniably useful, but complicated, expensive, and fussy to maintain. Wands focused magic, Master Burleigh had said. Not for the likes of them, or at least not Rufus, not so young, but a thing to know about.

He couldn't stop watching, as Lord Carillon bent carefully to each wheel, and cast a charm made of a murmured phrase and trailing patterns of light from the tip of the wand, beautiful enough to take Rufus's breath away. He was startled enough to jump when he heard the question a moment after the last wheel. "It's an enchantment to ... remind the ground what it's like to be solid. Under the fronts of the wheels, and a little at the back, for traction. Do you think you can help me give it a push if we get Gossip to give it a pull?"

Rufus nodded at this and then said "Sir, I can do the ground ahead. So the mare can pull on solid ground, not risk strain or slip."

Carillon looked up at this, approvingly, and there was a "Do that," that was all order, though he followed it up immediately with a "Please."

"Sir, yes, sir." Rufus agreed reflexively.

The other man nodded and went along to see about the mare, murmuring to her in a way Rufus approved of and got her straightened out, and then there was a "You push here, and I'll get her moving and then come help you push."

The mare pulled with a good will and kept going once Lord Carillon ducked back to push, but it was only with both their shoulders against the back that they got it moving.

Rufus heard he horrible squelching sound as the mud filled in, just before he went ankle deep in the mud and got stuck himself.

It wasn't the mud that got him, so much as what the mud meant. He faintly heard Carillon move to collect the mare, and he fully expected he'd be left behind. Who'd notice, a peasant in the mud? But then Carillon was coming back, with a "Some mud. Here, give me your arm, don't mind about the muck, the muck cleans, here we go."

It was practised, so practised, and in that moment Rufus knew. "Been in a trench, sir?"

The silence after that question was so absolute, not only Carillon but the forest around them, so quiet Rufus could hear five beats of his heart, drum-loud in his ears. And then, quietly, "Yes. You?"

Rufus nodded. "Buried in one. They got me out. Luckier than some."

There was the flash of recognition, and a quiet, "Me too." And then a, "Can do better by you than that, now. Give you a ride, and a chance to clean up?"

Rufus made a face. "Sir, Ytene's the other way from my cottage. And you've the mare to see to."

He dared a glance up, and he could see the man's calculations, barely hidden under the surface, trying to make the maths come out in a way that would give him noblesse oblige and also be sensible, and failing to add it up.

Finally, Carillon sighed. "No, you're right. Give you a ride up to the crossroad, then?" and Rufus nodded. "Crossroad."

Carillon got the mare sorted out. He rummaged in his pockets to give her a small lump of sugar, and then they rode in silence the half mile up to the crossroads. When Rufus climbed down, Carillon produced a silver piece -

enough to buy him a week of meals and a beer or two besides - with a "Thank you. Maybe we can do each other a good turn in future if you're up my way. I'm still getting settled."

Rufus ducked his head, and then added a "Safe journey, sir. The north road gets mucky on the left."

Carillon drove out, laughing, with a "Ta for the reminder." He drove off, nudging the mare into picking up a nice little trot now the cart was lighter again.

FOUR

TRUE EYEWORTH

Nanny wanted to keep the children with her as a special treat for tea, one of her sisters coming to visit. That meant Ferry was free to go on her own to market day, and linger.

She paused in front of her mirror, then tucked an early rose from the bud vase on her dresser into the ribbon of her hat. That done, she went off to find the pony cart that was waiting for her by the stables. It was a more than pleasant day for a drive, and faster than walking. She found herself humming as she pulled up to the village inn and could turn the mare over to the stable hand there.

"Back in a few hours, George," she told the innkeeper. "There'll be a couple of deliveries coming, for Cook, like we discussed." He grunted and nodded, but it was the easiest way to get flour and cheese and half a pig, not to mention any other heavy goods, back to the house. She was glad enough to drive the carriage if it got her out of Boar Court for an afternoon. It was hard for her to get into too much trouble with a well-behaved horse and cart.

It was a greater pleasure to walk through the market

stalls. More than one person spotted her pendant and asked her a question or two. She enjoyed settling into a proper chat with one of the woodworkers about magics worked into boxes and chests. For protection, for preservation, for storage options. She half-remembered a theory about rotating the storage spaces in a trunk and promised to look it up. The library at Boar Court was fantastic, built by earlier generations buying to learn new things, not just because they looked good on shelves.

She took her time wandering up and down the main street, going to each place, checking the other stalls, before she turned into Pross's shop. Pross was busy helping another customer, that was a good sign, and Ferry waved a hand. "Happy to browse! Sure I'll find something to suit."

Ferry settled in the back corner to peer at a book on the local flora and fauna and some of their folklore. It was a fabulous book, leaving her trying to decide if she could manage the coins for it this week, or needed to hope it didn't sell. She'd heard the door open and close again, the murmur of Pross and her customer, another set of footsteps, then there was a "Pardon, ma'am."

She startled, nearly dropping the book. She twisted around to see the man from last week, suddenly very cautious.

"Ma'am?" he said. "Sorry. Didn't mean to startle. Mrs Gates told me you were looking at the - natural history, the word is?"

She nodded, not quite trusting herself to speak. He continued, "She asked if I'd have a look at - at that book, actually, see if it seemed accurate. The illustrations."

Ferry blinked again. "Pross - Mrs Gates did?"

Rufus nodded. "May I? If it's not a bother?"

She handed the book over and then wasn't at all sure

what to do with her hands before tucking them behind her back. Rufus flipped carefully through the pages. He was someone who respected books, she thought, but perhaps he hadn't had a lot of them to handle, the way he was cautious with it.

Rufus paused at an illustration of a dragonfly, the iridescence shimmering in the flickering of the moving image, before he turned a few more pages, making a tsking noise. And then a very pleased one, as he read for several pages, biting his lip in concentration. She stood, silent, watching him like she watched skittish deer in the forest, until he looked up, grinning.

"See this? It's got that line of rose pink, on the underside of the orchid, that's just about right, lots of pictures don't. And this, here. About the ponies. This is quite a good description of the breeding lines, much more detail than some. I don't know the all of it, but it's promising. Gives you more to learn from, rather than just a basic summary."

He was glowing with it, having found something that delighted him. "Here, sorry, you should get this."

She took the book, automatically, when he held it out and looked at the image. The illusion pony looked up from its grazing, and she couldn't help reading the text. She was several sentences in, when she remembered where she was and looked up, blushing, suddenly shy.

"Mrs Gates said you were looking for a good guide. That's a pretty good one. Pictures better than most, the folklore's the stories people tell. And it covers a lot. See, here, there's pages on the wandermists. And here, this chapter, it talks about the stories about a white hart? There's rumours there's one about again, you might see it. Um. Ma'am."

"Ferry," she said, automatically, after a moment. "Ferry,

please. We're near enough the same age. You don't work for me."

It startled him. "That's not proper - I mean, people will say things."

That got her, sharply. "People will say things for me thanking you for keeping Caelus from harm." She's quite clear on this. "I need my job, or I'd be -" A pause, then. "Pardon. I've got a streak of stubborn a mile wide, my Aunt Annonia says. She likes it, no one else does."

He tilted his head, as if he was taking his turn at watching some creature in the Forest. "I'm Rufus, you're Ferry. Um." And then he made an embarrassed face and a "Come here often?" He clearly didn't know what else to say, but as soon as it left his lips, he realised what he'd said, how it'd come out.

That made her laugh, and reply, "Pross - Mrs Gates - is a friend. I like reading. I work for the Bainbridges, out at Boar Court. I'm governess to their children. They're with Nanny and her sister today. Pross knows I was looking for a book about the Forest. I started - um." She blushed. "October last year. And then it was a bad winter, and we couldn't get out much." She felt she was stammering.

He nodded. Winter storms, mud, flooding of more paths than usual. "And you - went to Schola?" He gestured at her pendant.

She nodded. "You?" she asked. She almost continued, but then stopped, letting him answer instead. She didn't see an apprenticeship seal or a journeyman one, but lots of people didn't wear one.

He shook his head. "I was apprentice to Master Burleigh. He did cart building and boxes, making things. Nothing fancy. Carts or magic. Solid, though. But he - went to the War, when I was fourteen. And I went a few years after that."

She frowned. "Oh." She was not sure what to say for a moment or two, then "I'm glad you came home."

That startled him. It was an unusual thing for him to hear, she could see that instantly.

"Lots of people wonder why me. Why not their husband or brother or father?" His voice wasn't bitter, but tired.

"Oh." She considered. "I'd think there's no easy answer to that."

He looked up, with something like relief. "No." Very simple, his answer.

She let out a long breath. "I went to Schola, yes. I learned quite a few things. I wasn't allowed to study some of what I wanted, like magical beasts. materia." He looked puzzled, and she offered "Making magical objects, or using physical things to hold magic."

That got a nod. "That the fancy word for what Master Burleigh did? Some of it?"

She nodded. "I don't know much about the carriage parts, but - there are things to make more space in something, or protect things. If you do it in clothing, with the thread, you can make people look better, make things fit them better, keep them healthy. Aunt Annonia makes jewellery that does specific things."

He was about to ask something else when the door opened. They both heard "Oh, Proserpina, dear, I was wondering, have you seen dear Ferry, I was hoping to catch her, I've something she simply must take to Nanny Ogden."

Ferry let out a frustrated sound, made an apologetic noise at Rufus, and then called out "Here, Mrs Talbot. Just a moment."

Rufus nodded and murmured "I'll stay here. She doesn't like me at all." Ferry took her book, holding it carefully, and walked out, with a clear "Good afternoon, Mrs Talbot. Pross, I would like this, thanks for the chance to look through it properly, and the help evaluating it. Could you wrap it in brown paper?"

It took a while for them to get Mrs Talbot to leave. By the time they did, it was past time for Ferry to head home, to beat the dark. Pross looked at the light, and said, "Look, how about Cammie and I come out tomorrow, after church? Make a picnic of it, or they can play inside?" Ferry agreed, and they set the time and slipped out the door.

Ferry looked back up the street, once, on her way back to the inn and the pony trap. She saw Rufus slipping out of the shop to head the other way out of town. She turned and made her way home, wishing she'd had a chance to say goodbye to him properly.

FIVE

BOAR COURT

The picnic was not entirely satisfactory. The children were fine. The weather was fine. The blanket was fine. The small man-made lake was fine.

Pross was chatty for much of it, through unpacking the basket of treats Cook had put together, and getting the children sorted. They were off now, by the trees, in the small fort one of the older groundskeepers had built for them. Not at all parentally approved but what their parents didn't know wouldn't hurt anyone. Ferry thought it was good for them to play freely.

She couldn't, however, stop thinking about the conversation yesterday. Rufus had been so delighted at the book. She'd been up far too late reading it, savouring it.

She had started with the chapter about the ponies, about introducing different bloodlines to the Forest, how they'd been monitored. The book was recent enough to mention the number of horses killed in the War. There was a chapter on how the magical folk in the Forest had kept enough breeding stock back the bloodlines would recover. Given time.

This morning, before the children were her responsibility, she'd read from the beginning. She'd taken in the chapter on the history of the New Forest, and the one laying out the overall climate and flora and fauna that flourished here.

This wasn't her home. She knew, logically, that she was only a visitor. She was here on sufferance as long as the Bainbridges choose to keep her, or until her family convinced her to marry someone they approved of. Not a palatable future, either way. She was stubborn, but there were a lot of her family, just as stubborn, and she knew when she was outnumbered, junior, and not going to be listened to.

Except maybe by Aunt Annonia. Who was also rarely listened to.

She must have been wool-gathering for some time because it took Pross tapping her foot and a "Ferry, did you hear a word I said?"

Ferry blushed. "Sorry, I was thinking. Ta for the book. I've read three chapters already."

Pross nodded. "That Rufus Pride thought it well done. And not just the obvious parts, but the things people leave out or get wrong." She waited a moment, then there was a "So what did you think of him? He asked me how we'd met, once you left."

Ferry laughed. "Did you actually tell him?"

Pross shook her head. "Not all of it. Just that you'd come in looking for a book, and we got to talking."

It wasn't wrong. Caelus had been a horror before they'd sorted out how things worked for them. And Pross had been a useful bribe. They'd agreed that he would do his best for her. In return, she'd make sure he got to read about things he enjoyed, and do things he found fun, and they wouldn't tell his parents.

Just like she wouldn't tell them about Cardea climbing trees and riding astride on a pony. Or half a dozen things that were not ladylike but entirely reasonable to learn. She wanted Cardea to have what she had not.

She was wool-gathering again, and she startled to find Pross looking at her. "He's, he's all right. He's got a poor reputation, but a lot of it's..." Pross paused. "You're not used to tiny villages, are you?"

Ferry shook her head. "You know where I come from, smaller than Trellech, and it's not London, but." She paused, trying to describe it. "Insular, but not like a village? More like Bath, I guess, in stories?"

Pross nodded. "There've been magical villages mixed with the others for centuries, in the Forest. Those who can see them do, the others just go around. Never through." She wiggled a hand. "But there are still expectations."

Ferry nodded, cautiously.

"And Rufus's family. They're magical. But they're not supposed to be too strong or skilled at it. No one gets much formal training. Women learn to keep the milk sweet, heal little things, save dropped stitches and mend socks. Nothing showy. Men learn to use their magics to - make things sound. Sound barrels. Sound smithing. Sound joinery and masonry and whatever. Sound horses."

Ferry opened her mouth, closed it, and then a "But not - school? Or maybe even apprenticing in magic?"

Pross nodded. "Mind, I didn't understand this until Octavian explained it." Her late husband.

Ferry nodded again, not pressing.

There was a pause before Pross said, "You and I, we had

the chance to learn a lot of things. And they felt - not very connected, at the time. I know it did for me. But they gave us lots of choices. Options. Ways we could go. For Rufus, people like him, there was one path. Maybe two or three, but closely related. Farm. Craft solid reliable items. Live in the Forest, like their parents and grandparents and great-grands."

Ferry chewed on this. "Ok." She says. "He said he apprenticed?"

Pross nods. "All right, so I know this only because there was a lot of gossip about it when we moved back here, took over the store and the holding," she says. "When he was about twelve, his magic built up. It does in people, I guess. And there was a.... Well, I guess the other villages still talk about lightning and dragons and all sorts of things, trying to make sense of it. Lots of light, lots of sparkle. It looked like magic's supposed to look, in all the stories, not just the little bits, we do, but a wave. Like an aurora."

Ferry blinked. "That's. That's not normal."

Pross laughed. "No, no it's not. Startled just about everyone. And a day or two later up shows Master Burleigh. He was the main crafting master around here, turned his hand to more complicated magical items? Abundtia Carter, with those boxes you like, she learned from him, and Lorcan Stope, who does the pots that grow herbs well, did too."

Ferry nods. "Those boxes are complicated," she says. "I was asking her some about them the other day. Several layers of magic worked in, and materia choices."

Pross nodded. "So. Master Burleigh didn't take a lot of apprentices? And he was getting on. He must have been over seventy? The age most people would slow down, have a decade or two easier. But he showed up and told the Prides he should have the care of Rufus unless Rufus made it into one of the Five Schools. Rufus didn't. I gather he didn't do well on the written exams. So when Rufus turned fourteen, he went off to live with Master Burleigh, proper apprenticeship, signed and sealed."

"And then the War." Ferry's voice was very quiet.

"And then the War. Our Ministry drafted Master Burleigh early on. He held off as long as he could. He was seeing to things here, said he had a new young apprentice, all that. But they sent him over to France in 1915, and..." Pross paused. "No one's sure what happened. The official story is gas, but no one believes it? Something horrid, magical, but we don't know what. They aren't telling."

Ferry had to look away. There was something in the intensity of Pross's voice. "Oh," she said to fill the space. "And that meant Rufus was on his own?"

Pross nodded. "Neither fish nor fowl, and only fifteen, maybe sixteen, himself. No one else wanted to take him on. No one else had time. Everyone who could was doing something for the War. And if they weren't, they were keeping things going on the farms and the fields and the mills and... all that. His brothers went off to fight. Didn't come home, one by one."

That made Ferry shiver. "Oh," she said again, helplessly. "And then he did? Went off?"

Pross nods. "I guess he had a huge fight with his parents. He was still young. Might have... put it off. Gone into something that took more training. He'd always been a good reader, I guess, since the village school days. Some parents petitioned the War Office, about their last sons. If the others had..."

Ferry shivered again. "So he went?"

Pross nodded. "And he - was very lucky. More than just chance. Not just him, but people around him. One battle, they were supposed to be at the front, got sent somewhere else, the last moment. His mum said he was in a trench collapse, but in a pocket of air, they got him out safely. No real damage. Just how the boards had come down, and the muck and the mud. Him and the... dozen or two, nearest him. Horrible, still, but it didn't kill them."

She paused. "There were rumours, a gas attack, the wind changed. Blew away from where Rufus was. More things than that. Each one could be chance, but - not so many added up, all together?"

Ferry shivered for a moment. "That's." She considered. "I remember hearing something about it. Magic doing that. Especially if it's not - trained. Focused. Directed. But I don't remember where. Just sort of bubbles out. And if the person means well, it does good. Like a puppy looking to please, not always sensible good?"

"That's an image," said Pross. She stretched out on the blanket, watching the children for a moment. "Mums tell stories. I mean, when they get together. Watching babies, children, for their magic. Wondering what it might mean when they grow up."

Ferry was quiet for a minute. Then, she said "My family worries about that. I'm..." She hesitated, then went on. "I'm good at the theory, but not much at doing things. My brother's worse off. The things I can do are the delicate ones, Aunt Annonia says. The ones about a small amount of power, precisely used. She suggested clockwork magic, once, but my parents wouldn't find me anyone to apprentice to."

"That's a waste. You'd have been good at that. Not that you're not with the children, but that's intelligence, too, and the charm pieces your aunt makes for a few things. I'm good at the things about keeping order. It's handy for business, mind. The indexing enchantments."

They digressed into different types of magic and how they played out in the world. Ferry enjoyed speculating over what Cardea and Cammie and Caelus might have a knack for. It was much more amusing than either the frustrations of Ferry's parents or thinking about the War.

SIX

TRUE EYEWORTH

May Day dawned bright and cheerful.

Ferry had been up for ages already. Up in time to get dressed in the dark, by a lantern, to meet up with the groom and maid and gardener to take the larger cart into town. Nanny Ogden was having none of that. "You young people get up and greet the dawn, I've done my time and well past."

Ferry had laughed, but there was something potent in the darkness. Mysteries. The unknown. Possibility. Rattling down the road, with Harold driving the ponies, she could see why someone older, settled, would stay in bed.

Not for her, though. She wasn't sure what this May Day would bring, but she wanted to be there.

Her parents would have scolded her for it. Most of her aunts. They recognised the changes of seasons all the magical families had their own little customs for that, passed down and brought in by marriage. Honey-sweet candles for the winter solstice, and mead for May, bonfires to stoke the family magics. Some families had blessings for orchards, some for sheep, some for children, some for more complicated kinds of increase and abundance.

Those things were pleasant. Who didn't like apple cakes, or gathering flowers out of green fields?

But here in the dark, bumping along without distraction from her thoughts, she thought it was all missing something. It felt as if much of what they did was going through the rites and magics by rote, like memorising texts in school to give the right answers. It didn't have a spark to it. There was no room for the unexpected.

When they pulled up to the green, in the village, the bonfire was all set up. Not lit yet, that would happen only once the sun crested. But the musicians were tuning up, people beginning to let their voices free. She could hear bells, see glimpses of trailing ribbons on staves and decorations, dark against the hints of dawn. She slid down, murmured to the others she'd make her own way home, and went off to do a circuit of the green.

By the time she'd circled, taking a steaming mug of tea, the dancers were forming up. There was the song before the dawn, different in each village, and she'd never heard this one before. It had the sound of hooves in a drum beat, a riff of a pony's whicker, snippets of birdsong. She closed her eyes, listening, so attentively.

From that, the sounds shifted, changing, repetition of the main melody after repetition, growing broader and grander, voices and the instruments they had. It built and built until someone saw the sun. A great cry went up, from the hundreds of people who'd come out of the dark and stepped joyous into the light.

Someone grabbed her hand and pulled her into the circle dance that was forming up, and she laughed. The dance left her breathless, in the best way, new and different, like everything was possible. Another person bowed to her, and she curtsied back, and they were off for another dance. These were simple steps that passed partner to partner, moving through everyone there, until they circled back.

This was the necessary magic, the true magic, she thought. And that magic done, she could curtsy again, and take herself off to a bench, to watch the more complex dances, the village ones she did not know. People came around with food, more to drink. By the time the sun was well up, she was decked in three chains of flowers. Someone had tucked a shimmering magical rose into the coil of her hair. She spent a little time watching someone tell hilarious illusion stories, local legends of magical beasts.

When the gathering finally settled down, people easing out to their own particular groups of family and friends, she knew enough to leave before she felt entirely left alone. She murmured a few things to people as she passed them, taking the street out of town. She aimed for a particular little field half a mile toward home, where she could find peace with a book for a little.

It wasn't too long before she heard footsteps behind her, and then a cough, and "Pardon, Miss - Ferry. We seem to be going the same way?"

It was Rufus. He was dressed for the dancing, he must have been there, in a vest of deep green with many different coloured ribbons hanging off the shoulders. They must mean something she couldn't interpret. She paused, turning back toward him, with a "Joyful May!"

He smiled, though as if it was not joyful for him. "Did you enjoy the celebration?"

She nodded. "I've never been to a proper village one. The ones at school, but they were different. It was - it felt real. Like everyone.. Meant it."

He tilted his head, and there was a "Huh." Something complicated and uncertain.

She turned a little, standing on the road, unsure what to do now. Part of her was vibrating, buzzing, still wound up from the dancing and the swirling community magics. She jumped when she heard a rustling in the woods to the side of the road and a strange undulating musical call, unlike any bird she'd heard before.

Rufus startled too, and then urged, "Oh, come this way." He instinctively reached out a hand for her. Ferry took it, and he tugged her along, over into the woods at the side, following a narrow deer path.

Ferry had just thought enough to be glad she'd worn ankle boots under her skirts before she was entirely too busy ducking branches and hopping over roots. Rufus never quite dragged her, but he urged her on, saying "Come on, you'll like this, it's brilliant." It was minutes before they ended up in a grove deep in the forest, a space filled with dancing glowing shapes.

"Mirabiles." Rufus murmured. "Miracles." They were magical creatures, rarely seen, and much like some forms of religious art. She watched the bright formless shapes rising and descending, dancing and swirling about six feet off the ground. Rufus drew them over under a large oak. Before she realised it, she was leaning a little against him, entirely enraptured in what was going on, the beauty and the freedom.

Rufus pointed out particular flourishes to her, never taking advantage of that leaning, just continuing to hold her hand. The mirabiles twirled and sang and danced, and Ferry couldn't stop watching. The more she watched, the more she wanted something, as fiercely as she'd ever wanted anything in that world, and she breathed it out. "They're free."

She shivered, immediately after, with a "Sorry."

Rufus squeezed her hand. "Don't be. Remind us what's possible, they do. What we can reach for. More than - the daily muck and grind."

Ferry was silent for a long moment, and then she looked up at him, and whispered, "Thank you for this. For. For." She ran out of words.

Rufus shifted, to face her a little, leaning against the tree with one shoulder now, leaning forward, watching her intently.

It was overwhelming, suddenly. The dancing and the singing and the morning she'd had, and all the magic buzzing in her blood, wanting to find a purpose. She flushed, and looked away, then shyly back up at him. "I. I...." And then she impulsively stood on her tiptoes and kissed him on the lips.

She'd kissed a boy before, but this was nothing like that at all. He inhaled sharply, against her lips, and then there was a hand around her waist, bracing, shifting a little, tilting his head as he kissed her back. He didn't press, didn't push beyond what she offered, but she was so aware of his height, his shoulders, his strength.

It was intricate, this, as complex as the dancing they'd just been watching. She stopped thinking about it, and just let herself choose, shifting to let her back brace against the broad trunk of the oak, to arch up a little on tiptoe. His hand flattened against the wood, and his hips slipped against hers, and she could feel a different hardness against her stomach, which made her whimper against his kiss.

He immediately shifted back, a "Did I - is something -" that was all concern, and she shook her head, so insistent.

Ferry looked down and blushed before she looked up. "I - it's grand." She looked away. "That sounds stupid. I - I just. I felt."

A glance down again, and he blushed this time, deep red. "Oh. I can - I can move?"

The impulsivity grabbed her again, and she shook her head, sharply. Her hand slipped around his waist, doing her best to encourage him back where he'd been, with a fiercely whispered, "Please kiss me."

He let out a low moan as if he'd no idea she'd ever say that, pressing her against the tree. He let her feel that strength and solidity, making her feel utterly secure in where she was. When she opened her mouth to him, his tongue pressed in, teasing, encouraging, and she took a little to realise his whole body was moving with that. His hips arched, and she could feel him, his hardness, against her. She was trembling, like she was flying, and she never wanted it to stop.

It didn't. He pulled away to let her head rest on his shoulder. It was not long before he murmured "May I touch you? See if you like something?"

She didn't know what to expect, but she nodded, murmured, "Yes," in his ear. His hands lifted, his left moving to brush the outer side of her breast, angling so he could get his hand around and under, cupping it under her dress. She startled herself with a loud moan, something entirely unlike what she expected of herself, pressing into it.

This drew a laugh from him, and a more urgent shift of his hips. "Oh, Merlin's... Merlin's cap, you like that, oh, yes, oh, so good," his words trailing off into a murmur of incoherent pleasure. He explored her reactions, what touches over her clothing made her gasp or shift or arch, alternating with deep kisses and nibbles at her ear.

Finally, regretfully, he murmured, "I - want more, m'lady." The term slipped out of him, and she shivered, and he immediately pressed a little closer. "But not here, not right now, not like this. We're. It's May Day, it's the dancing, it's... my blood is on fire, wanting. And you deserve. Better."

Ferry was trembling now, barely able to hold herself up, but when he looked at her, she nodded, carefully, like the world would shatter if she moved too fast.

He watched her, then said, "I should walk you back to the road. I'd... we're not near anywhere I could get a cart." He pressed his hand into the tree, to push himself away, doing his best to breathe evenly and failing.

Ferry had to let her eyes close, and when she opened them, a dozen breaths later, he'd backed up a little. The mirabiles were gone, now, just little trails of light dissipating, and she reached to straighten her dress and hair, instinctively twisting it up and pinning it.

He waited, patient, until she was done, and then held out his hand, with a "Let me escort you." They walked in silence, hand in hand, back to the road, and down to the turn up the drive to Boar Court. He bowed and murmured, "I'd - like to talk to you again. If you want. Maybe you could let Pross know when you'll be in town?"

Ferry nodded and then blurted out, "That - again, please. Sometime. Sometime when we can," before she turned and ducked up the drive.

SEVEN

THE ROAD TO TRUE EYEWORTH

Rufus watched Ferry walk up the drive. The house was hidden behind the trees, but she paused just before the road turned, saw him waiting, and waved once more. He waved back and waited until she was out of sight, before turning away himself.

His head was spinning, he felt drunk. He'd never expected that of all the things this morning. He'd seen Ferry at the village green, caught glimpses of her dancing, and singing and clapping, enjoying herself. He hadn't expected the rest of it.

But she'd been the one to kiss him. Not a thing a well-bred woman would do. Only she had, and a good bit more beside, and the memory of it made him hard again, instantly. It made him blush to think of it, and weak in the knees to think of the other things he'd like to do.

He'd been with women before. Not many. Janet, from the village, when he'd come home from Master Burleigh's for the last time. Beth, on his last night before shipping out. Those had been urgent, sharp, needy things.

This had plenty of need, but there was more than that.

He wanted to understand her. She wasn't like the people he knew, men or women. She knew things he didn't. She wanted to learn things he knew like breathing, about this place, these plants, these animals. And oh, he could feel the pulse of her magic.

That was the first thing Master Burleigh had taught him. That everything had magic, running just under the surface.

Some people had tremendous power, a blazing fire of magic waiting to rise. Some were clever, they could follow the twists and turns of complicated spells and make them come out just right. Master Burleigh had talked about precision, accuracy, rather than strength. And then there were people who kenned the magic, who could follow the ebbs and flows, like the river or the seasons, could read the moods and mind of the magic and shape it, deliberately.

Master Burleigh had been clear. Rufus had power. But they'd only got as far as tamping it down, so it didn't lash out. He'd had a few fights, when he was twelve or thirteen, when that had happened, and they scared him stiff. It had got out of control again, after the War, when the nightmares and the daytime terrors grabbed at him. When he drank too much. When the drink didn't help one bit.

Rufus knew it scared other people, but it hadn't scared her, the surges he could feel. She'd gone to school, the fancy school, surely she knew what he was. They must have had words for people like him, wild ones, dangerous ones. Surely someone must have warned her off people like him.

Her magic, though, he could feel that. Delicate, like an embroidery needle, like his Mum used to do, each stitch placed precise and accurate, to make a picture of something fine and new. Stitching in the old charms, the ones the family knew, to keep a shirt sound and clean, the thread marking out letters much older than books.

Like vines, their kissing had been, reaching out, making shapes and growing, getting stronger, the more they shared with each other.

Rufus had felt like he wasn't alone for the first time in years.

And yet, here he was. No job. Barely a home, good chance he'd lose it when the taxes came due. No choices. No one to hire him. He read and wrote better than most from the village, but that wasn't much compared to clerks and secretaries and scholars who'd gone to school or had a proper apprenticeship. No prospects. No connections.

No real skills except his back and his labour. Not with so many horses gone and nobody trusting him with the ones that were left.

They had reasons, he had to admit. He'd not been the kind of man worth trusting for years.

A sensible lady wouldn't want him. Couldn't want him.

He turned away, finally, to begin to trudge back across the village road, back toward the cottage, buried deep in the other side of the woods. Not so far from Ytene, and that made him think, longingly, of that chance meeting on the road. He'd wondered if there might be a job in that, but he'd been a willing hand and shoulder, that was all. Men like Lord Carillon didn't think to have men like him turn up again. He might get a coin or two, but then nothing.

He was nearly back at the turn to the village when there was a "Hey. Pride. Hey."

Sharp and hard, and he looked up. Johnny Alder. He paused, nodded. "Hey."

"Need a bit of work, d'you?"

Rufus paused. "What kind of work?"

"Bit could use your ungodly luck."

Smuggling. Rufus was sure of it. He didn't say anything, he let Johnny make the first move.

"C'mon, Pride. Good coin in it. Know you're past skint."

Rufus let out a puff of breath. "Got a place to talk about it?"

Johnny sketched a gesture. "The old charcoal camp, down by Docken's Way, two hours?"

Rufus nodded. "Two hours, there." A nod and he took himself off, sidetracking through the village to use his precious coin to pick up a bit of bread and cheese for his supper. George at the inn was kind, gave him a bit extra. From the gossip, people had been generous with the donation cup this morning.

He got to the rough hut twenty minutes before time, and found a stump. He started slightly at any of the sharp sounds of branches, like a lost pony, until he saw Johnny come up the path.

"Just me. For now. Unless you decide. Your word on your magic you won't tell what I share."

Everyone knew Johnny was a smuggler. The trick was catching him at it. He didn't do the night work, he did the daytime, seeing what paths were clear, what roots or rocks or pits had changed since the last time they ran that route.

Someone else - he didn't know who - got the cargo. And someone else got it out of the Forest to ship or cart or portal, wherever it was going. Someone else sorted a cargo for them to bring back, taxed goods like rum or tea.

Rufus paused, then nodded. "My word on my magic, I won't tell what you tell me here and now." He felt the twist in his magic, before he saw it, the little whisper of bells, the flickering light that passed over his hands and face.

Johnny settled on another log and watched Rufus. "You know what I do, aye? We could use someone like you. I've been watching you."

Rufus looked back, steady as he could. "And what sort of someone would that be, then?"

"Steady. Not like to lose your head. Lucky as all get-out. Good with creatures."

"I've no real skill with magic."

"More than most who'll be there."

Rufus couldn't quite argue with that. "What's in it for me?"

"Five parts."

Rufus blinked. That was a lot. Five parts of a hundred. He didn't know how many people were involved. Then, letting the suspicion Johnny would expect into his voice. "Five parts of how much? And what do you want for it?"

Johnny laughed. "Oh, can't give you a number. Biggest run we've done since before the War, though, and the last one near this big, three parts was enough t'buy a proper house, common rights and all, at the forest edge. Be all civilised."

There was a twist to his tone that made Rufus wonder suddenly if Johnny had seen him with Ferry. If he'd realised that Rufus was suddenly much more interested in not just surviving but finding something more. He made a noise, the next step was signalling he was thinking about it, not being hasty. "And what's the cargo?"

"Can't tell you that, either. Creatures. Nothing too deadly. Some plants. Salamanders. Usual liquids."

Rufus made a noise, not satisfied. "Not too deadly's not enough of an answer." The usual liquids would be a mix of alcohol, distillations, and potions, then.

"Right then, we've salves for the thing that might, but it

comes out of your share. Don't think it's likely, we've moved them before. Mix of things."

Rufus considers. "Plenty left in the Forest, what you're taking?"

Johnny looked up at this. "Why do you care?"

A shrug. "Forest takes it out on people, get too greedy. You remember Old Edward when I was a kid? No desire to end up like that, me." That had been a source of stories for half a decade, how he was found, near-mummified in a clearing, no sign what had done it, but all the cages of arrinsocks broken open, their paw prints scattering out in the ground and disappearing back up into the trees.

Johnny waved it off. "Ballocks," he said. "Stories to scare kids. But no. Not the last of anything."

Rufus nodded, though he wasn't sure if Johnny was telling him the truth. He tapped his foot. "When would you need me, and how long?"

"New moon, on the twenty-sixth. Couple of hours to get the cargo to the sea, couple of hours back with the new cargo. Back by dawn. Ponies, no carts."

Rufus nodded. "What'd my role be, if I said yes?"

"Steadying the ground, over the bogs. Helping with the ponies when we're not in a bog. Nothing you can't do."

Rufus grunted. Steadying the ground was one of the first things he'd learned, and it came easy still. When he concentrated. "Nothing underground?" He couldn't quite keep the nerves from his voice.

"We've got Bolton, he's worse than you. No caves. Not this time. No tunnels."

Rufus nodded. "Let me think on it. When do you need an answer?"

Johnny shrugged. "Market day, for the planning."

"At the pub, then?"

"Aye. The usual way."

Rufus nodded and pushed himself standing. "Got a few things to do before dark. Ta, Johnny."

That got a nod from the other man, and the uncomfortable sensation of Johnny watching him as he turned his back on the camp and made his way back toward home.

EIGHT

THE PRIDE FAMILY COTTAGE

Rufus paced the cottage, turning every three steps to avoid knocking his head on this beam or that. The rain had started not twenty minutes after he got home. Now it was a pounding storm that was soaking everything and dripping down through too-bare thatch to make a puddle by the table.

He kicked a bucket under it, shifted his path around it, and kept pacing.

Too many options. Rufus had never been good with choices. He knew he wasn't quick-witted, able to see all the holes and dangers.

He could take Johnny's offer. Johnny knew what he was about. There was a risk to this, or they'd not have brought him in, but also a big reward if they brought it off. And they knew he was desperate enough to take it, and if he took it, he'd do his best. He'd never been accused of shirking. Not after the first few fights, anyway. They might overestimate what he could do, but if they needed the steady ground, maybe not.

He could turn Johnny in. Or near enough. He'd sworn

not to share the names, and where they were meeting, but there were only so many places they could go from that meeting spot. If they needed him for the boggy bits, that meant two or maybe three routes. He knew how large the cargo had to be, to pay that well. Where it might be hidden. He knew the Forest. If he turned and told the Guard, they'd find them, like as not.

That was the way to never live in the Forest again. Stay and turn up dead some unkind night, or exile himself. And the Forest was all he had left. Even if he couldn't join the May dances, he couldn't bear to never hear the music again, to lose everything that way. His roots ran too deep here to bear leaving.

He wanted to find some third road, but he had no job, no future. Smuggling was the best he had.

Rufus shook his head. His parents would have despaired of him. His Mum had wanted her children well out of that. She'd come from a town family, come to live in the depths of the Forest for his Da. She'd taken to the rough farming, the cycles of the sheep and the pigs and the ponies and the chickens, all their coming and going.

They'd not had much room, ever. A bedroom for them, the kids up in the loft, but they'd had more than enough to eat, and to share, and laughter and music. He knew that wasn't how it was for most magical folk, who wanted their space, but it was what they'd had. If he and his brothers woke each other up, well, they coped. Nothing else for it.

His Da had been in with the smugglers before Rufus was born, before most of the kids were. Mostly keeping the ponies steady as they carried cargo, from what little he'd said. But they'd still heard stories. This run or that, this trinket or that. It had seemed a grand game, once. Now, he couldn't get Da's voice out of his head, one night when it was late, and they were talking around the fire, not wanting to go up into the chilly loft.

Life's not like stories. May seem grand to go out in the dark and bring home enough money to keep Mum in food and cloth and pretties for years. But the money runs out, and then what do you do? They'll be asking more of you, and more. And they'll own you, sure as any of the Families would if you worked for them. Decide for yourselves, do you want to live free or not?

Rufus had had plenty of time not free. Too much war, too much death, too much being ordered into the impossible.

Another turn around the cottage. And another. Then kicking a bucket under another leak.

Ferry had seemed pleased with him. But she wouldn't be if she saw how he lived. She'd seen him at his best, cleaned and tidy, doing his best to keep his worries off his face. Ferry had seen him with all the ribbons and finery he had left, showing all the pride he could muster. She'd turn away, the same scorn on her face as near everyone else, if she saw this place.

It was clean enough and tidy enough, but that was all the good could be said about it. The only decent things here were from his parents. The blanket on the bed was getting threadbare and worn, the cushions on the surviving chairs. His clothes were all getting thin in the elbows and knees and seat without his mother's tending. And only a few paces across, any direction you went.

Smuggling could change that. Give him time to figure something out. If he was in with the smugglers, maybe one of them would give him steady work, during the day. Maybe the reason he'd been struggling was that they didn't trust him. Thought him too uncanny. Maybe this was the chance to prove he wasn't. That he could be steady, a man like them.

Or if he was uncanny, at least a helpful sort of uncanny.

He blew hair out of his face, frustrated. What did he have to work with? A small herd of ponies, out on the Forest right now, though they came by regular. A tiny herd, just the yearlings that had been too young to take for the war, or born just after. They'd lost their best mares that way.

There was a cart he couldn't use, the axle needed fixing, and that was well beyond his skill with the tools he had.

A cottage which wasn't doing too well at being shelter. He'd tried to keep up the cob and the thatch like his Da had taught and the protections on the clearing and the hearth like his Mum had. He'd stopped borrowing books from Mrs Gates, because he couldn't be sure they'd be safe from drips and leaks and mold and awfulness. And he couldn't afford to pay if it got ruined.

The last bucket, under another leak.

He knew bits of it. He'd helped his Da mend the cob, learning how there was the layer of runes tucked out of sight. He knew they added strength, kept in the warm, kept out the rain. He'd renewed them last fall, he could do that again.

There were runes for the thatch, but he'd not learned those. He was still young enough then his Da had worried about him falling, reaching for where the runes were buried in the rafters and beams. And everyone had warned him against doing much magic until he was trained up better. His Da, his Mum, Master Burleigh, his brothers.

His Da had thought they'd have plenty of time for him to learn things, that summer, before the war. That he'd have years to apprentice and learn and grow up. He didn't. None of them who'd been young then had.

So what did he know? Ah, that was the question.

He knew how to stop his magic exploding out. Mostly. Or at least, he'd learned how to release it deliberately in a burst, when it built and built until it felt like it was scratching at the inside of his skin.

If he didn't take up Johnny on the offer, he'd have to do that soon. He'd have to go find a quiet place in the Forest, nothing around to hurt, and let it rush away into old trees and old rocks and old bogs that could absorb it. Master Burleigh had taught him that, at least, and except when he was in the trenches, with no way out, he'd not lost control of his magic since.

He knew about horses. Not as much as his brother. Jasper had apprenticed to a carter, one of the best in the Forest, and he'd come home bubbling over with how he loved it. Their Da had shut him up quick.

But one night, before Jasper went off to war, they'd gone out to the meadow, in private and out in the open. Jasper had sat him down, told him that their family had a language, a way with horses. That they weren't the only ones, Jasper had met others now, cousins, far up north. Their Da hadn't taught Rufus, Rufus was meant for other things, but Jasper wanted to pass on some of it. Just in case. For the family. So Rufus would never forget where he'd come from.

He couldn't do what they had done, his Da and his eldest brothers, but he had a knack with the ponies. Only there weren't many horses here to do with, and plenty of other people had the skills and a lot more experience. Better trusted. They all knew Rufus hadn't had the training, besides, because he'd gone to Master Burleigh.

Everything he'd learned had been hard won. He'd woken up one day, out in the dirt outside, with Star standing over him and nuzzling his hair. He'd not even made it in the house staggering home from the village and the pub, no memory of more than that in his head. She'd run wild since his parents died, just like he had, but there she was, with a memory of him, and she'd let him train her up.

That, he was proud of. That was why he'd kept on. She was a sweet-tempered mare, and smooth-gaited, responsive but not flighty. Before the cart had broken, he'd had a better time of it. He'd been able to haul boxes and people back and forth to the portal down in Beaulieu, or take the occasional message on horseback.

So what he had was Star and the rest. A cottage that leaked. No real knowledge of runes. An ability to manage a bog or a road if it got mucky. And no options but Johnny's offer that would let him stay where he belonged.

NINE

TRUE EYEWORTH

"Pross, do you have time?"

Pross was sitting behind the desk, and it had obviously been quiet most of the last few days - there were no new receipts on the spindle. The odd tear in the brown paper wrapper was the same as last market day.

Pross spread her hands. "Made of time. Come up, I'll put the sign in. Cammie's down the street with that Delphie." A new girl in town, eldest daughter of a merchant setting up a new line in housewares.

Ferry waited for Pross to turn the sign around, so it let people know to ring the bell if they'd a need, and bring the cash box upstairs. There was the usual bustle as they went upstairs, threading through the boxes of stock waiting to be sold and stepping over the ginger cat who sprawled at the top of the stairs. Ferry settled in her preferred chair in the little kitchen and waited until Pross had the kettle on.

"I might have got a little carried away. May Day."

"Traditional time for it. You going to have a Candlemas child, then?"

"Not that carried away!" Ferry was entirely shocked. "What... you thought I'd...."

"People do. Frequently. That's why it's a common sort of thing. Not every year, but often enough." Pross was entirely matter of fact about it. "There's a theory about it, actually."

Ferry couldn't resist leaning forward a little. "Theory?"

Pross finished with the initial fussing and came to sit while the kettle boiled. "First theory, that the village magics - the individual dances and songs - are meant to attract people who fit with that place. Can benefit that place. That the people who find it attractive, they're the ones ought to stay. It's why some folk stay away. They're scared the song will have changed for them, and not sure what to do with that."

Ferry chewed on her lip. "That." She paused for a moment. "I thought it was gorgeous. Grand. Amazing. I felt - part of it. Part of something, period. Like I haven't, for a long time. Like I did in my house, at school, being in the right place, but not - I don't feel like that with my family, most of them. Or the seasonal rites there."

"So that's not the right place for you. And that's a good thing to know, now, isn't it?"

Ferry winced. "I'm not sure what I think about it," she admitted after a few moments.

"Consider it a theory, then. So that's one part of it. And we have a piece of information, that you liked our celebration. I admit it was rather good this year. Even considering. New lines in it, somehow. Possibilities."

Ferry smiled at that. "You liked it too."

Pross nodded. "I did. It's why we moved back here. But that's another story. So. There's a theory that the different village magics, they're meant to draw people who can..."

She stopped. "You know why we turn the ponies out on the Forest?"

Ferry blinked. "That's a change of subject."

"No, no it isn't."

"Um. So you don't have to feed them?"

Pross laughed. "Well, there's that. But that's not why we turn the stallions out."

Ferry considered. "I - hadn't." She blushed.

"We turn the stallions out free, and the mares, so it's a natural mixing. Not us, saying this mare and this stallion. But them spreading it around a bit. Whatever it is they choose, however it is mares and stallions choose things. But we keep doing it because it's good for the breed. Strengthens it. It's called outcrossing."

Ferry tilted her head. "I still don't quite understand? But I never had magical creatures at school, so."

Pross settled back, then the kettle sang, and she said, "Minute, let me figure out how to explain it." She busied herself with the fussy little gestures of pouring tea, and the milk and a smidge of honey, and a half piece of quickbread each and a smear of fresh butter. "There. Properly Forest fed, that is."

"You were going to explain?" Ferry prompted.

"I know your family's got horses, that you ride. You've seen how some breeds, the ones that get fashionable, people breed for all sorts of things. Hounds and cats, too. You go for the flashy colours but lose the sweet nature. You go for elegant legs, and they founder too often. It's a trade-off."

Ferry nodded, cautiously.

"Outcrossing means - you give up a bit of control about what you get. But you bring new blood in. Makes the next generation more hardy, often. Brings out new skills. If we were talking children, might be a new knack for a kind of magic, or a gift for something. Harder to tell with a pony, since they can't tell you what's in their head."

Ferry tapped her fingers silently on her mug, waiting for it to cool. "So you're saying there's a theory the village magic is doing that? Only with people?"

Pross shrugged. "Encouraging. Not forcing. But yes. I do think that, sometimes. Or at least it's opening a door to possibilities we might shut out at other times,"

Ferry closed her eyes. This was easier if she didn't have to look at anyone. Even if the person was Pross. She could feel her friend waiting patiently. Finally, carefully, she said "Rufus came up to me, on the road. I don't think he was looking for me, he was looking for something else? And we were talking, and then he, he spotted mirabiles!" The awe of them was so sharp in her memory. "They were…"

Pross murmured,. "Seen them once, only the once. They're such a thing, sweep you off your feet."

Ferry had to cough though she still didn't look. "He took my hand, and we were running through the wood, to a meadow he knew, and they were dancing. That's the right word for it. So gorgeous. We watched for a bit, by a big tree, one of the oldest oaks, I think. And I was… I turned to thank him, and then I really wanted to kiss him and so I did."

This gets a little snort from Pross. "Well, see, that's a man with nice manners for you. How was it?"

Ferry went deep red, she could feel it, the flush of her skin and the heat. "It was grand," she said into her lap.

"It was…" Pross let her voice trail off, expectantly.

"Grand, all right? More than grand. Kissed me back, and I wanted it, and it felt so good, and… lots of kissing, and him against me, me against the tree, and he touched me, a little, asked first, my - my chest."

There's another laugh from Pross, and "Oh, Ferry, love,

I'm not laughing at you, just the situation. So. It was good, and you wanted more?"

Ferry nodded, and she snuck a quick look at Pross, who was grinning broadly, then opened her eyes fully. "It. I've never, anything like that? Kissed a couple of boys at school."

Pross grinned. "Rufus, not the same kind of grabby, then?"

"Not at all, really strong and careful, and he was - " She stopped, with a "No fair!"

"Just trying to get a proper sense of the landscape. So. You liked that with him. You'd like other things? How... I don't know your family, what would that mean?"

Ferry waved a hand. "Mother taught me the things about first times, long ago. And Matron, up at school, I went to her class on the protections you need. Our family..." She pauses. "There's power in a maidenhead, but that's not what my family's bartering with, I know that much. Or they'd not have put a bedding trial in two of the contracts."

Pross made a sour face. "That, now, that's a misery. You'd not told me that. For their benefit, I assume, not yours. I suppose it means you can make sure he's not horrible, but if they're not really letting you have a choice about who they make a contract with."

Ferry nods. "That'd be why I threw a fit and sulked and refused. That it wasn't about me, not really, for all they said it was."

There's a long pause, then Pross says "So. You could try things with Rufus. Without it being - without it risking everything else? Your family and everything?"

Ferry had to look down again, she knew she was blushing. "I could. Only. How could I ask? And it's not like I could bring him back to Boar Court."

"Well, no. Nanny Ogden's a lovely nursemaid, but she'd put anyone right off bedsports for a month."

This made Ferry laugh, and if it had more than a bit of hysteric edge in it, sharp and uneven, Pross didn't comment on it, just nudged her tea mug. "Drink up, love. Tea'll settle you."

They were both quiet for a good couple of minutes until Ferry said "But how could I... do things with him and then go back to my family? And someone, probably someone horrid. Who's interested in me as a symbol."

Pross considered. "Well. Wouldn't it be better to have a few good memories? Have made a choice for yourself? To look back on?"

Ferry looked away. "I. I don't know. I really don't."

Pross considered for a moment, then said, "Well, here's another thing for you to think about. The Prides, there's a rumour they've the Horseman's Tongue. Don't know if Rufus does or not, but his family, all kind, far back as I've heard tell. Good with their hands. Picking up cues."

Ferry blinked at this, not at all sure what to do with it.

Pross was about to say something further, and then there was a bell from downstairs, and she stood up. "Take your time finishing up, or you can read if you like? I'll go see to that. But I will say I regret the sex I didn't have a lot more than the sex I've chosen to have, one way or another. You might do with a little more impulse in your life, see how it suits you." And with that, she went downstairs.

TEN

NEAR BOAR COURT

It was clear out when Ferry got free for her afternoon off. She had a good three hours that day, time to walk a fair bit down the road. Several times she thought she caught a shadow moving, something just out of the corner of her eye, but each time she turned around it was nothing, not even a deer or a rabbit.

The fifth time she thought she saw something, she looked, turned away, then jumped as she heard a cough from the woods and a "Psst. Ferry." She couldn't figure out where it was coming from as she looked all around. "It's me, Rufus. Over here!"

He was standing tucked into a grove of trees, deep in shadow. "Path and a bit of a place to sit. Do you - can you - will you?"

It was the 'will you' that got her, the hopefulness in his voice. She nodded, glanced up and down the road, and there was no one to spot her. Once she was well in shadow, he took her hand, tucked it into his arm, and escorted her down a narrow deer path, maybe fifty feet from the wider path she'd been on, up over a crest of a low hill and down the other side, to a small meadow where there were a few flat stones, and a blanket stretched out. It was pinned down with rocks, and she recognised a batch of Pross's scones and a little cream, in a small dish.

He ducked his head. "Pross said you liked her scones? There's cream, too, but no jam, sorry."

She smiled back, shy and skittish, but nonetheless fascinated. "I do. Where are we?"

"A meadow. Quiet. No one comes here much in spring. The edges, they get pigs in the fall and some mushroom hunters. Now, though. Not much. Deer."

"It's not the deer I worry about."

This made him laugh. "No, they're not a worry." He walked her over to the blanket, waited for her to settle down, and then sat cross-legged opposite her, not venturing more contact, but watching her.

"The last time we met - did I..." He stopped and flushed. "I'm sorry."

She tilted her head, watching him. "You thought I'd be angry?"

He nodded. "Well-bred woman like you. You've..." He stopped, tried again. "I was very forward, ma'am."

"Ferry." She was insistent. "Ferry. You did nothing I didn't ask and agree to."

He looks away. "It was May Day. It takes people funny."

"Pross explained. Some end up with child. We did nothing so..." She stopped. She'd been about to say so lasting, but what they'd done was lasting plenty well so far.

He caught it, "Nothing so...?"

She blew out a breath, up into the loose strands of hair

around her face. "Nothing so lasting. Only. Only I've kept thinking of it. Of you."

There was a sudden flashing grin from him. "Have you, now? That seems fair. Can't stop thinking of you." She looked up at him, then away, blushing, and he laughed. "Oh, there's a picture."

She was quiet for a long minute, reaching to break a scone, spread it with the clotted cream. "Pross must approve of you. The cream's not her favourite thing to make."

This startled him, and then he said, "You've known her long?"

Ferry shook her head. "Six months? Give or take. I got here in early October. They told me she was the best source of books for the children, which she is, unless someone goes to Trellech or London or something. And then market days, when I could get in, or she'd come by to visit." Any of the much larger magical communities would have even more books, but her employers certainly would not bother with such things.

Rufus nodded. "She. She didn't really have a friend. People she knew. Not friends."

Ferry considered this. "I wondered. She's... not from here, I know."

Rufus shook his head. "Her husband was. They came back, a year and a half ago. He died a year ago. She's... keeping on. Not easy."

Ferry nodded. "I know the - shop isn't doing very well. Or well enough, anyway."

Rufus murmured. "True for more than Mrs Gates."

Ferry let out a long breath. "We should.... I don't know much about you. Your situation. I don't know what you know about mine."

"You're a governess. The boy and girl?"

"Cardea's ten, and Caelus is eight. Their parents travel. They hired me last year, their last governess couldn't." She stopped. "She wasn't suited to the village, I guess. Nanny didn't like her either."

"And Nanny is?"

"Nanny Ogden. She was nanny to their father, back when."

He was quiet, and then said, "Not a world I know. Any of it."

Ferry looked away, not sure what to say until finally, she said, "I don't know much about yours. I'd like to."

"Brutal." It came out before he could stop it. He could hear her inhale sharply and caught himself. "It. The world's not been kind to me or mine."

She ventured a, "You're alone. No family?"

"Related - distant but related - to half the county. Not so they notice."

She nodded. "Pross told me a little. Your brothers."

"My brothers went in the War. My parents in the Scourge. Been just me for - three years." Three years, six months, twenty days, today.

It was completely quiet for thirty seconds, and then she said, "I'm so sorry." Just that. Earnest and clear and not trying to make him feel better. Strangely, it did. And she wasn't trying to get him to make her feel better about his loss, either.

He looked up, to find her watching him intently. He coughed, then said, "Thank you." She tilted her head, curious, and he continued. "People. Make it about them."

She exhaled and said, "It's not like that for me. But it sounds like - you miss them. Loved them." She sounded wistful about that, but he was too lost in the memory for a moment to do anything about that.

Rufus was quiet for a moment, nodded, and then there was a long pause. It was one of those places where the conversation could go two different ways and the way it was going was a choice. He inhaled, then chose boldness. "Why are you here? Do you have family?"

She nodded. "Well-bred family. Rather a lot of them. One of the First Families, do you know what that means?" He nodded. "They're - we don't have a lot of money? Or a lot of magic, these days. But we've got plenty of habits about who we are, how we do things. Expectations."

Subdued, she added, "They want me to marry someone of the - right sort of family. Money. Bloodlines. I didn't want to. Not the one they picked last time."

"Not the one last time?" He wasn't sure what to make of this.

"I'm twenty-five. He is near sixty. He's had two wives. Both died." A pause, then she continued, "I'd been... promised to someone. From when we were tiny. He was five years older, but he died in the War. I think it'd have been all right with him. I knew him. He liked me well enough. We were friends. But not what they tried after that."

Several things in this horrified Rufus. "They'd just - marry you off? You wouldn't have a say in it?"

"My father's supposed to be the one to decide."

"That makes no sense."

"That is the way the First Families do it." Her voice was dry and detached.

"They hunt for sport, too." His was full of utter scorn.

It was that which made her look up. "You - don't - you must hunt?"

"For food. For protection." He ventured to reach a hand to cover hers. "You're your own person."

"Not to them." Now she was the one who was fatalistic.

"I'm a chess piece. Connections and marriages and opportunities."

He made a frustrated noise. "That's not right."

"Not much choice."

He squeezed her hand, then "Do you - like them? Love them?" He wasn't sure how to say this at all.

She had to think about it. "I - I think they want what's best for me. What they think is best. I don't think they're right, but I don't think they want to hurt me. I knew some people at school. Horrid families. Much worse than mine. And there's not much choice, these days. Eligible men."

Rufus winced. "Well. If they only want to marry you to someone in his fifties, twice your age, Merlin."

Ferry snorted. "Well. Lord Carillon's not very likely to ask me to a grand masked ball any time soon, is he?"

Rufus startled at this. "Why him?"

"One of the most eligible bachelors in the First Families? Every letter from my aunts has some hint on how to catch his eye."

Rufus laughs. "I met him. Week or so gone. Carriage got stuck in the mud, helped him get it free. Treated me decent, not like many. Not sure that'd help you."

Ferry shook her head. "Not much, no. Not good at that kind of thing."

"What -" He stopped. "Sorry."

"Go ahead, ask."

"I was wondering. What you... thought you were good at."

"The delicate magics, mostly. Or at least I'd like to be. But a lot of it takes apprenticing. Someone showing you things. I can sew, but embroidery turns to something flat in my hands. I can copy things, not make my own. But my family, they wouldn't let me study the things I was more interested in. Clockwork. Weaving."

He nodded and was quiet for a minute. Then, carefully, there's a "I'm thinking we should maybe talk. About a few things in particular."

ELEVEN

NEAR BOAR COURT

Ferry looked up, a little startled, and he shook his head. "I - you should know, the village doesn't like me." He caught himself. "No, that's not quite right. They don't trust me. And that's worse."

She blinked at him, confused.

Rufus took a deep breath. "My fam's been here for centuries. Way back to the Domesday Book, they say. Had forest rights. There's seven, all told."

Ferry nodded. "Nanny explained most of them." She counts off on her fingers. "Pasture. That's turning out ponies and donkeys, and... cattle, isn't it? To graze." Rufus nodded, and then a "And sheep are separate, though I didn't understand that part."

Rufus said mock-solemnly, "Sheep are very different, yes."

Ferry chewed her lip in concentration. "Mast, which is turning out pigs in the fall. That was when I first got here, and one of the farmhands took me off to show me. They eat the acorns, and that's good for the Forest."

Rufus nods. "And good for the pigs. And good for bacon and ham, eventually."

That made her smile. "And there's... oh, I can never remember the word. It's wood, though. For fuel? Estuary. No, that's a river. Estonia. No. Country. Estivate. No, that's a verb, and it's also not right. Begins with est."

He took pity on this though the string of words made him smile. "Estovers," he said, cheerfully.

"Estovers," she repeated, "Estovers. Wood for fuel."

He nodded. She counted off on her fingers. "That's four. Um. One's for clay, but I forget that word, and I guess it's not that common now? And there's one for peat. And then there's one for yew."

Rufus nodded. "Clay is marl, and you're right, not used much. People used to get peat turves for fuel, and that's turbary." And then a "Yew. The yew's a thing they use in making magical things, isn't it? That's yewbote. Only magic folk get that one."

Ferry settled herself more comfortably on the blanket. "How do they explain that, I wonder? Or do they assume people won't notice?"

"It's specific trees, and they - it's the same magics that make it so you can't find the villages? You just don't notice those trees."

"Huh." She tapped her fingers. "So your family - had all of them, then?"

"Sometimes we've not had pigs or sheep. But yes. The others, all, technically. Though taking yew needs training, bit of magic to harvest it right, and no one - no one my generation knew it." He got quiet again.

Ferry was watching him, very attentive. "You - will you tell me about them?"

Rufus turned away for a moment, to watch a deer

venturing near the meadow, to take a breath or two. "Haven't," he says, finally. "Explained. To anyone. Wasn't anyone to tell. Except maybe Mrs Gates, and she knew it."

"I'd like to know. Please." He had to look back at her, at the earnestness in her voice. She was so young, in some ways, and yet so clear on what she wanted, in a way he didn't remember ever having.

"Mum and my Da were - they loved each other. Solid. Thing to rely on. Mum was from the village, Da was a forester family, way back. Four boys, a couple of years apart, each. We never had much, but Mum made it so it didn't matter. Da kept things together. Always had his hand to something. They'd be ashamed of me."

"Ashamed of you?"

He made a fist with one hand. "Cottage gone to bits. Mares barely trained, not like they should be. No real trade to turn my hand to. Were so proud when I apprenticed. Not like my brothers. They were strong, they were sturdy. But not - not magic like mine?"

"And you miss them all." It wasn't a question, just naming the thing he'd been dancing around. He nodded, still looking away. There was a shift on the blanket, and she moved, to settle next to him, in a little tangle of rearranging her skirts, to reach for his hand. "Did you like apprenticing?"

He had to look up at that, and nod. "It was. Every day, I learned something new. Important. Mattered. But we hadn't got through much when - he got called up. Tried to get out of it. Made people mad." He took a breath, then a growl came out. "He never came back. Barely could write. Family took his books and things."

"Oh, Rufus. And you didn't have anywhere."

He shook his head silently. She was quiet for a little, just sitting beside him.

"Seems to me there are lots of different ways to be alone." Her voice was soft like she was thinking through something.

Her comment startled him. "What do you mean?"

She shrugged. "I feel alone in my family, too. Different. Like I never fit. Not the same reasons you didn't, but - not so different." Her hands fiddled with a fold of her skirt. "I've an older brother. He'll inherit. An older sister, already married as she was told to. I'm supposed to marry well."

Rufus considered this. "And yet you kissed me. May Day. And you don't regret it?"

This made her blush, the question. "I don't regret it, no." She was quiet but insistent. "It - sometimes people play around. Before getting married. After, sometimes, too. Depending. On the agreements."

That got a very dry, "Not like the villages here, then."

Ferry shook her head. "Pross brought that up. No. There's magics, have to do with sex, but Matron at school taught us the ones to avoid catching a child if we don't want to. And there's magics to help when you want one. They're complicated, expensive sometimes, or just need knowing how to do them, and the knowing isn't simple? But they exist."

He frowned. "So what was the kissing, then?"

She shifted, feeling him stiffen and pull away. "It. No, please, let me try and explain?" There was a pause, her gathering her thoughts. "I wanted. I - no."

She stopped. "I don't want what my family wants for me. I want something else. The Forest, it fascinates me. May Day, the music and the dancing, they made me feel like I was in the right place for the first time since school. I'd been thinking maybe, somehow, trying to figure out how to go back there, work doing something, even though I'm not near qualified. But then I came, and I heard the singing and the dancing, and my feet went in the right places, and it felt whole again." The words came pouring out of her, tumbling over each other, as she tried to explain.

He stayed still, listening to her, and when the words ran out, he shifted a little to cover her hand with his. "And me?"

"You." Ferry paused, and this was careful. "I don't know. I honestly don't. You're very different from everything I've known. But." She paused, careful, trying to make the words come out, trying not to spook him like a deer or a pony.

"That's a good thing. And a thing that scares me. It's like standing on a cliff, deciding what to do next. But you listen, and you answer my questions, and you know all sorts of things I don't." She looked down, and then away. "And I'd like to see what we figure out together."

"So, not running off and having a romantic vision of what it means to live in a cottage, then?" His voice came out sharper than he meant to, and he squeezed her hand immediately after.

"Not like that, no," she murmured. "I'm trying to be sensible. Sometimes it's easier than others."

This made him laugh. "What does it mean, then?"

"Well." She paused, gathering her thoughts. "I have a job for at least a few months more. I don't expect their parents back until the end of summer at earliest. Nanny thinks you might not be as bad as the gossip suggests - I guess she knew your mother? And Nanny has a lot of influence with the household, just not my parents." He made a small startled noise. "That gives us time to do things like this. Have a picnic. Talk. On my half days."

"Which are?"

"Half-day Thursday, and all day Sunday. And some-times Nanny takes them Saturday afternoon so I can come into market without them. They're good children, really, but they want a lot of attention, and attending to."

"Especially Caelus."

Ferry was fondly exasperated. "He's more obvious about it, but - Cardea would lock herself in a little room, away from the world, if she could. And that's not good for her. I should know, I did a fair bit of it."

Rufus closed his eyes, leaning back on his free hand while he thought. "People are different. Like ponies. All sorts of layers and habits and things that make them up."

Ferry nodded. "Not at all simple. And children their ages, there are a lot of ways they could go. I figure I can do a bit for them, at least."

They sat quietly for a few minutes, and then Rufus murmured. "When did you have to be back?"

Ferry laughed, startling a rabbit who'd ventured to the edge of the clearing. "Two hours or so?" She undid the locket clock pinned to her vest. "Two hours. I'll set a chime for when we need to start back?"

He blinked at her. "Just like that?"

Ferry was startled. "It's not - um. Oh, I guess it is. I can show you, though?"

This drew a smile from him. "Later. Set it now, and we will do other things than chime magic."

It took her a moment to realise what he meant, and then she blushed deeply.

TWELVE

NEAR BOAR COURT

"Not chime magic." And then she got a thoughtful expression. "Other kinds of magic?"

Rufus blinked. "I was thinking - um. Kissing? Maybe touching? If you - wanted?" He was suddenly adrift in this conversation. Didn't she want more of that? Like May Day?

Ferry laughed. "That too," she said. "It. Um. If you want? There are kinds of magic make things - feel different? That apparently go with touching? One of the older girls at school taught me some of them. For eventually."

"What kind of different?" Rufus paused, then said "I didn't expect. Um."

Ferry considered, then said. "How about some of what we've done? Again? Then maybe other things?"

This earned her a huge smile, definitely one of relief. "Ta," he said. "Been looking forward to kissing you for days."

She blushed, uncertain what to do next. He moved a little, and murmured, "You can stretch out, here, on the blanket? We can both be comfortable?" He didn't want to press her, but oh, he could see how she was, a mare learning to take to training, to trust his guidance.

She considered this and shrugged off her outer jacket. The sun was shining, it was not too chilly. He made an appreciative noise at the button-front dress she had on under it. Not at all smart or fashionable, but comfortable. He settled on his side, next to her, after shrugging off his jacket.

"There we go, then. You tell me if I do a thing you're not sure about, all right? And I'll ask some."

This made her bite her lip, and he paused, his hand halfway to her upper arm. She watched him. "You are being very careful with me?" Her voice was a bit uncertain.

"You said you'd not done much. And you're not a village lass. Different - growing up. Lots of ways, I'm guessing?"

"Lots of ways." She echoed him, trying the words out. "Lots of ways I didn't like much." She frowned.

"And May Day, we were, the magic carried us along. And it felt very good, but..." He paused, searching for words. "A lot of what I like is how you respond to me. Encourage. So if you're not being encouraging about it, that's not so good."

She considered this, then reached out for his arm, testing, and he smiled. "There we go, then. Lots of things we can do to get more comfortable. And we've not time enough to go too far. Also, not comfy enough or private enough for some things. But a little rolling around on the grass, quiet meadow, that's a thing. Especially in May."

That made her laugh. "Especially in May? Wouldn't do to go against tradition." She moved to run her fingers down his arm, feeling the muscle under the shirt, then brushing one of the darns, and she looked thoughtfully at it. "Your sewing's not bad, but, mmm." Clearly, a thing she'd do better given the chance.

He made a small noise. "Not my best skill."

Ferry shifted over onto her back and murmured. "I seem to remember kissing was a better one."

He laughed, and moved, stretching out beside her, hand bracing on the other side of her head, bending to kiss her, taking his time with it. She was eager for it, letting him get things going but following his lead, responding, pressing up into the kiss a couple of times. Opening her mouth to him. It made him arch against her for a moment, and she shivered, feeling something hard pressing against her.

He pulled away, bracing on his hand. "Pardon. Did you -"

Ferry looked away for a moment, blushing fiercely. "I. Um. Matron went over the... mechanics? At school. But not really. Does that hurt? Does it - is there something I should do?"

Rufus couldn't help laughing. "Oh, Ferry, love." It slipped out, the affectionate term. "Oh, you've heard stories or something, haven't you?"

"Boys at school. Swore up and down - not on their magic, but other things? Leaving them like that hurt. And I don't know. I don't know I'm ready for that, yet. But I don't want you to hurt."

Rufus moved a bit, to look at her steadily. "They wanted sex, there's no doubt about that. But that's not the way to go about. Men, we get hard all the time. Especially when we're young. By my age, needs a lovely lady in my arms, or looking my way, not just, y'know, thinking about something for half a second. But I had plenty of that when I was younger."

She was watching him, so earnestly. "So. What do... what's my part?"

Rufus bent to kiss her forehead for a moment. "We do whatever you're comfortable with. If you're comfortable watching me stroke off when we're done with what you're up for today, we could do that. You could touch me, bring me off if you wanted. Mind, suspect I wouldn't last long." Even the thought made him shift and suppress a grunt, the idea of her hand on him.

Ferry made a small noise, startled, and he murmured "Thinking about you touching me, love. Gets me going. Only if you want, though."

She wriggled her shoulders and said "Maybe that's a thing to - see if we can do?"

He took a long breath and nodded. "I'd like that. And you. Women can get - do you touch yourself? Have you, ever?"

This made her blush gloriously, a deep red that disappeared down into the bodice of her dress. It made him lean down and kiss her immediately, hungrily, and she responded to that as freely as any forest nymph might. He broke the kiss for a moment to murmur "Oh, yes." In her ear. "Just like that," before devoting the next few minutes to a thorough exploration of all the ways kissing her was wonderful.

When they came up for air, she was flushed in a rather different way, her hair coming loose, and her eyes wide, and a "Mmm. That's why people like that?"

"One of the reasons." And then he remembered what he'd been saying. "Women can ache with wanting, too, I'm told. Not so direct as men, I guess, but if you do, you can use your fingers, same as I use my hand. Or I'm glad to assist if you permit."

That got another blush, but it turned into a laugh, and she drew him down again, kissing him again. Then she was working a hand to try and begin and undo his shirt and expose more skin. He let his hands drift to her bodice, with a "May I?" in her ear.

When she nodded, he began to undo her dress, pulling back so he could kiss along the line of her skin it revealed. He let his fingers brush and tease, then expose her breast, then the other, and reach to touch them. She arched as his hands moved, into them, but she was moving beyond words, he could see that.

"Ah, there we go, love, you're grand, there." The rhythms of the endearments he'd heard from his parents came so naturally to him, the pace of how he'd gentle a mare, ease her into trusting. "There we are. Feel so good, love, how is that for you?"

She was wide-eyed, watching him, trembling, but shifting against his touch, her nipples hardening beautifully. He took a breath, then a "Let's see what you think of this..."

He bent to suck, closing his mouth around her, drawing on her. As soon as the pull began, she moaned, quite loudly, arching her body, her hips moving, legs spreading, opening up to this, to what she was feeling, entirely unabashed about it and trusting. And that, oh, that he found the most arousing of all. He took his time, sucking and kissing before switching to the other nipple, lingering there, letting her shiver and arch and whimper at each touch and kiss.

It was only because he wanted to show her new things that he drew back, to see her spread out on the blanket, decidedly different than the tidy proper young lady he'd first seen. He reached to brush her cheek and then murmured, "So. May I take myself out? Do you want to try touching?"

THIRTEEN

NEAR BOAR COURT

Ferry nodded, wordless, and he murmured. "You watch, then." He took a breath and she could see how his jaw clenched, his shoulder twitched. He reached to unbutton his trousers, letting them slip lower on his hips, untying his smallclothes and slipping them down. "Here, you watching?"

She blinked at this, then stared. It was nothing like she'd expected, despite the illusion diagrams Matron had used. The real thing was rather more solid. Reactive. Red. Hard. Clearly very hard. She swallowed once, then again, before she reached out a hand, carefully, and a "I - what do I do?"

Rufus bit his lip and said "Like to go off real fast. Know a charm to clean it. Or point away from us, the grass?"

It was hard for her to look away, to look up and meet his eyes, but she nodded.

"Kneel up here, love, next to me, so you can use your hand."

She moved around, awkwardly, on her knees, half-covering her breasts with the folds of cloth. Now they were at this point, she was all fumbles and uncertainty.

She got on his right side, then reached her hand, and as soon as her hand curled around him, he groaned. It was loud enough to startle deer in the forest, "Fuck, oh, fuck, that's good."

She startled at the swear, and he was immediately reassuring. "It's good, it's good, please, Ferry, please. Move your hand a bit. Head's sen..." She had discovered that herself, and he bucked in her grip.

Ferry looked up at his face for a moment, and then settled her left arm around his hip, to better brace. She closed her hand around him, and then she was lost in his reactions. She could feel how his hips were arching under her touch, how he was swelling in her hand. She could hear his breath coming faster, a whine in his throat. He was doing his best to hold off, she thought, when he cried out again, loud and unmistakable. Ferry felt his cock pulse, again and again, shooting off into the grass. She held on until the end when he was growing soft in her hand, then gently released him with a little startled noise.

He sank back to sit on his heels, hanging out in the air. She was flushed with the exertion and the newness, and not sure what to do next.

He sucked in a breath, then said "Want you to feel like this. May I? Touch you? Under your skirts?"

She shivered, but she nodded, wanting his direction, not sure what to say to that. Saying yes to this was so tempting, but also a very large, very new step.

He caught something in her mood, and he was right there, his voice gentle and reassuring. "Stretch out on the blanket, love, like we were. Going to reach and touch you, suck a bit on your gorgeous breast, know we both like that, mmm? Make you feel good. Like you did me."

That got a smile out of her, and she rearranged herself,

then moved her hips to make sure he could get enough space to work under her skirts. He grinned down at her. "That's the thing. There we are."

He stretched out beside her again, and took his time at her breasts, letting his hand wander and tease. Resting on her stomach, then her hip, then down her leg, then drawing up the folds of her skirts. Teasingly, his hand moved up the inside of her legs, keeping her focused on his mouth until he traced with his thumb.

His hands were rough, she could feel his touch catch on her skin once or twice. But he knew what he was doing, and after a moment he undid her underthings and found a spot that made her moan.

What he was doing, how he was touching her, it was shaking everything she'd thought. She'd heard girls giggle and laugh, but this was something different, forcing her to think of nothing but the pleasure. She could feel her body jerk, then shudder, and he settled in, to do those things again and again. He murmured to her like he might a horse he was training, easy and confident and glorious.

He shifted his body against hers to steady her, teasing and tormenting her until she finally shattered. Then she was shivering and crying out in a pure clean sound of pure pleasure. He kept touching, through the fading shudders, until she was limp in the aftermath, then stretched out beside her, arm across her waist.

She lay quiet for a good few minutes, and then murmured, "See why the boys were wanting. If it's like that."

This made him laugh, cheerful. "Well. Doing that takes a little learning. Women, take a bit more skill than men, usually. Though, mmm. You were grand, love. Touching me." He was a bit worked up again already, and he knew she could feel it.

"You've... done things before?"

He was quiet for a moment. "I have. Two women. It's Janet you have to thank for this, teaching me how to help you find your pleasure. She did her best to teach me as much as I could learn."

Ferry was quiet for a moment, thinking about how she felt. That he'd been with someone else before her. "Is she in the village now?"

He shook his head. "Married, someone up in Norfolk. Friend of her family's. Comes back for holidays sometimes, but not often. I haven't seen her since - before the war."

She stretched out against him better, contemplating what to say, and then the chime went off. "Not enough time to try again. You - you will be all right?"

He moved to kiss her lips, lingering at it. "Promise." Then he pulled back, with a "We should tidy up. Get you back to the hall."

Ferry nodded, and once he sat up, did the same and pinned her hair back into place, by feel.

He watched her, amazed. "No mirror?"

"It's my head. I know where things go."

That made him laugh again, then keep laughing, and she grinned back at him, finishing pinning up her bun before she worked on doing up her dress. She did the buttons up wrong the first time and had to try again. By that time he'd got himself in order, and could stand, reaching down to help her up. "Walk you back to the drive?"

She nodded. "I'd like that." Very clear, very simple. She helped him pack up the blankets.

He led her over to a pony, tethered under the trees nearby. "This is Star. Best of our ponies." The chestnut mare was golden copper where the sun hit her coat, with a broad white star on her forehead and a narrow blaze like a trail across the sky down her nose.

Ferry held out her hand, carefully, to be sniffed, and Rufus murmured "Here," pressing a bit of carrot into her hand. The mare mouthed it off her palm tidily and then whuffled. "She likes sugar better, but I don't have that to spare."

Ferry smiled at that, and said, "Oh, you're well-mannered, aren't you?"

"Do you ride?" he asked after a moment. "I didn't... do they learn to ride where you're from?"

Ferry had to smile at this. "I ride well enough if the horse is well-trained. Mother made me ride sidesaddle, but our groom taught me astride, too. And then we did some with horses at school. But I haven't much the past two years or so. A lot of our horses went to the war."

Rufus grimaced. "A lot of the Forest ponies, too. Too many. She was just a yearling then, they spared her." He reached to settle the saddlebags behind Star's saddle and untied her. "Let's walk you back to the drive."

They walked in silence before they both started speaking at the same time. "Can I..." "Do you..." They laughed, then he gestured at her. "Lady first."

She coughed, then said, "Um. What does - us mean to you?"

Rufus stopped for a moment, and the mare stopped as well. Then he said, "I - don't know yet. Honestly. There's a lot I like about you. Your curiosity. You - getting things about the Forest. Wanting to understand it. And you're smart and you like what I say, and your smile. And -" He let his glance dip down to her chest for a moment. "Other attributes."

It made her blush again deeply, and duck her chin and look away. Then he turned serious. "Can't offer you much. Not just you. Anyone. Next to no money. No prospects. No - nothing. It's. I can't make a plan, about anything in the future, with that."

She nodded, and she walked along in silence for a minute or so before she said. "My parents want to marry me off. Someone old and awful." Laying it out, tidily, like a proof in geometry. "I'm here because I won't. I like the children, but I'm not sure their parents will like what we've been doing. As much play as formal lessons. The kind of play. That sort of thing. And I don't know what's going to happen next week or next month or next year."

Rufus let out a breath. "All right." He says. "So what does that mean?"

Ferry reached out, after a moment, for his free hand. "I like trying things with you. Tricky to find private time. Not in a meadow, anyway. But no one... my body's mine. My family can pressure me to marry, but they can't make me. There are lots of things wrong with the First Families, but that's not one of them."

Rufus tilted his head. "That's..." He stopped. "Village, in the village, people don't unless they're courting. Mostly. Girls, anyway."

Ferry considered. "I think it's maybe partly because the First Families, there's a fair chance the woman's as good at doing things magical as the man, as well-trained. Maybe in different skills, but that doesn't make her someone to cross?"

Rufus could see the logic in that. "So. You can take care of yourself?"

Ferry shrugged slightly. "A few things, maybe. Though you've been very much the gentleman so far." He winced at the term, and she offered. "If you've got a better label for it, I'll use that."

"Not to hand, but I'll think on it."

"Does that mean we should plan something for my next day off? I can get clear for Market Day afternoon, I think, if one of the grooms comes in to take the carriage back with the heavy goods."

Rufus nodded "I'd like that. I'll see if I can get free. If someone offers me work though…."

"If you get offered work, you take it. That matters." She was very clear on this.

By this point, they were almost up to the drive, and he said "I'll look for you at the market. If you don't see me, find a bench by the square, eh?"

Ferry stood on tiptoe to kiss him, not lingering where people could see, and then drew back. "Saturday. I'll look for you."

FOURTEEN

TRUE EYEWORTH

The next Saturday, Ferry was efficient. She had sorted the market day orders for the house and had them taken to the carriage, so they would be ready when the groom went back.

Duty done, it was time for her enjoyment, so she was making her way along the market stalls, a word here and a word there. She caught sight of someone she didn't recognise. Someone well off - he was wearing smooth robes of fine wool, not the local homespun. Rather nicer than even her family would wear, especially out to market day.

The man turned, in profile, and she made a noise. The woodworker's wife glanced down the row and snorted. "Looks just like his older brother, he does. That's our Lord Carillon, holds Ytene, now. Back in the county, and to stay, I gather. Been buying things up, here and there. That there, he's talking to James 'bout a saddle, I believe. Been asking other things about the village, where to get things, who does what kinds of work. Do you know him, miss?"

Watching distracted Ferry enough she was jarred back

to the conversation. "Not directly, no. I met his brother once or twice. Before." Before he turned up rather mysteriously dead. "Lord Carillon - this one, I mean - wasn't he doing something awfully exotic? Travelling somewhere, in the back of beyond?"

"I wouldn't know about that, miss." She added an impish, "Not like the likes of him tell likes of us about their travel plans. And he's only got one or two staff up at Ytene yet, and they don't gossip. It'd be good for the village if he did more hiring, but he's taking it slow, he is."

Ferry watched the man pay for something, with a few coins, but go away empty handed. Work on the saddle he left on the saddle rack, maybe. She tapped her fingers on the stall and said "Can I ask what the village'd like? From him?"

The woman considered, weighing the question, and then there was a slow, drawling, "Well, miss, that's a thing for the village. How was it, your May Day?"

Ferry looked up sharply, and she could tell the answer here would change things, but not how. "I - I loved how it felt. All of it. The singing and the bells and the tradition, even the parts I know I didn't understand. How it all fit together. How people had a sense of what was right, at that moment, and shared it."

It came out more effusively than she meant, but the woman smiled at that, something easing. "Ah, now, that's a thing." She gestures. "That's a man wouldn't have found the song right before." Before the war. Before his family died. Before so many things changed. "But maybe he does now. Didn't dance, him, but he came down proper, before dawn, laid his branches for the fire, left his coin, knew his part."

Ferry tilted her head. "Thank you," she said. "I think I understand. Something changed for him when he came back, and this is a place for him now? That can be his home?" And then softer, shyly. "I - understand how that feels now."

This gets a beaming smile from the woodworker's wife. "There's a sensible girl, then. We'll be seeing you next week, then? Maybe with the children? I've a toy or two they might like."

Ferry nodded. "Of course, ma'am." She turned away, making her way down the street to the square, and finding an unoccupied bench to settle on. Pross wouldn't be free yet, she'd said, so Ferry drew out the book she was reading and settled in to enjoy the spring and the quiet and the lack of immediate obligations. It was perhaps twenty minutes later when she heard a quiet "Pardon?" and looked up.

It was Lord Carillon, and she immediately made to stand. He waved a hand. "No, please, don't. I am being horribly improper, but several people have told me about you. You are Feronia Wright, yes? Of the Cornish Wrights?"

She nodded, and extended her hand, politely. He shook it, rather than either kissing the air above it or letting his magic brush hers, as some people did. It made her like him rather a lot more already. "Miss Wright," he said, promptly. "I am Geoffrey Carillon. Recently returned, oh, I'm sure the gossip has caught up with me. I'm back to take up Ytene again, as the last of our line. I believe my grandfather knew your grandmother rather well at school. No, great-aunt, wasn't it?"

His phrasing charmed her. "That was Great Aunt Mellona, wasn't it? They had a shared interest in bees. Auntie always felt she needed to live up to the name."

Carillon broke out in a broad grin. "Well, I heard a

fascinating story about them going after a wild hive, got into one of the bohort field trees, and you know what a bother that could be. And getting rather stung in sensitive places."

This makes her smile back. "Goodness, yes. She wouldn't tell that one when Mother was around, though. Made Mother very disapproving."

Carillon nodded. "May I join you for a few moments, then? Now we have established our introductions?" Ferry shifted over on the bench and murmured "Of course. Please, though, call me Ferry. Everyone does. Except Mother and Father."

That got a serious nod. "I am normally Carillon. Silly, but there you are, it's a custom."

She offered him a small smile. "I should probably say my family have been hoping I'd meet you."

There was a flicker of something across his face, and then he said "Well, I am delighted to have met you. I understand you're taking the Bainbridge children in hand. I know the parents slightly, but I know they travel near as much as I used to."

Ferry nodded. "They're good children. Clever, once you get them interested in something. I try to make sure they've got plenty of time to play and explore, too."

"Champion!" This was startlingly approving. "Lots of our sort don't get enough of that, time to figure things out on our own." And then his tone turned amused. "So, are your family hoping I'll sweep you off your feet? I am afraid I'm rather unlikely to oblige, and it's nothing to do with you or your virtues."

Ferry had to pause a moment to think through that, then she offered a "Sir?" that was curious.

Carillon spread his hands. "Well, for one thing, you're

what, twenty-five? I'm near enough forty. Hardly seems fair to you."

"My family's last attempt at a match was near sixty. Joachim Elder."

"Mordred's mercy! I hope that's not going forward. Entirely unsuitable, and age is the least of it."

Ferry blinked. "There's another reason? I didn't like him at all, but I didn't." She stopped, trying to figure out what to say.

Carillon shook his head and murmured, "It'd be improper for me to give details, at least to a well-bred lady I've only just met. Now, I'm quite familiar with a wide range of preferences, from my travels. I rather take the opinion that what two people decide to do together is not anyone else's business. Or more than two, for that matter. But Elder's the sort of man who wants his own pleasure and doesn't care a yew berry for his partner's. That's nothing I'd wish on anyone at all pleasant."

Ferry made a face. "He said he was being proper with me, but he insisted on kissing me, and it was awful." That came out of her in a rush, and then she blushed.

Carillon nodded, pausing for a moment to let her gather her composure. "I also dislike what I hear about his business dealings, but that's an entirely different sort of question, isn't it? Pity to marry someone for a stable future and have it collapse, though. I'm told marrying poor for love has its virtues - or at least rather a lot of books imply it's worth it with the right person. But marrying someone you dislike and then having the money go wrong seems entirely unfair on all counts."

"Not that my parents would listen to that argument. They'd assume I did not understand."

Carillon sketched a bow while seated. "If you'd like, I

will see one or two of your extended family over the
summer season, I suspect. I could put a word or two round
where they might hear. Mind, I'm not considered all that
reliable myself."

Ferry blinked. "Why not, sir?"

He laughed, and said, amiably, "Most of them think I'm
a fool. I don't dress well enough to be a fop, you understand,
but they assume I'm all pavo and travel and fun and games."

He shifted then, and she glimpsed the ring and the
shimmering white stone it held. She stopped and stared,
forgetting to reply. Carillon laughed, and confided, "I was
Owl, at school. Not what people who've met me since
think. But I like puzzles, sorting them out, especially old
ones. That's why I travelled a lot. One of the reasons."

Ferry nodded. "Horse, for me. I think maybe that's why
I like the Forest so much. Plenty of ponies."

Carillon smiled at that. "Quite a few, yes. I'm looking to
set up a proper breeding stable, among other things. Since I
need to be back here. And it seems to me that could absorb a
certain amount of problem-solving, at least for a while. And
I do play pavo. Might as well breed my own mounts if I've
got a farm and stables to do it on."

Ferry considered. "I'd think it'd be quite complicated,
really. And it'd take a while to figure out whether what you
were trying worked out. I mean, horse breeding takes years
for results."

Carillon nods. "In the meanwhile, I'm looking for
mares, and maybe a stallion, and then people to help run
the place. I'm still learning about the community here.
Who's reliable, who isn't."

It was about that point that Ferry caught sight of Rufus,
at the other end of the square, and couldn't help brighten-

ing. Carillon caught the shift, and murmured, "And who do you see there, m'lady?"

Ferry murmured "Rufus Pride. He's been telling me a bit about the Forest." She looked up to see quite a strange and confusing expression on Carillon's face for just a moment before he replied, "That's a name I've heard. Oh, he's coming over, good."

FIFTEEN

TRUE EYEWORTH

Rufus was frustrated. He'd come in to market mostly to see if he could find work. And to talk to Johnny, before he looked for Ferry. He hadn't seen her on Thursday, she'd sent a note saying Nanny wasn't well and she had to take care of the children. That she'd try and meet him Saturday.

Which he'd done, pressing into the crowded smoky pub, waiting his turn like a scolded boy, as man after man pushed in before him. He'd waited a good hour before he could get close enough to murmur "I'm in." Johnny had nodded, and made a dismissive gesture that hinted at later business. Rufus had slunk out, hearing laughter, sure it was meant for him. It had that edge.

He'd glimpsed Carillon while he was waiting. The man had come into the bar for a quick drink, and my, the topics had changed rather quickly. He tipped well, Rufus could see the glint of the coin. It wasn't until the door was well closed behind him and his posh robes that the less legal talk started up again. Not just the smuggling, but a little deer poaching, where to get a boar, the usual trade in tales.

Then it took him a good ninety minutes to make the rounds of who had work. Or who didn't. Something had shifted. To be honest, he knew what it was. Talbot had looked him up and down, and said "Not with the company you're keeping at the moment," and turned away. Peters had said "Not this week." And Mason was nearly friendly though the work would be gruelling. He couldn't turn it down though.

It wasn't until well after three he could make his way to the square and look to see if Ferry was still waiting. She was, but he saw, as he crossed to her, that Lord Carillon was with her, sitting at ease, talking to her. He said something to make her laugh, and Rufus bristled, feeling the jealousy gnawing at him.

A moment later, she spotted him, and there was a smile, lighting her up, and a little shy wave, before she said something else to Lord Carillon. He could only assume she meant him to come over with that, and so he kept going, setting his shoulders like he was back in France. He came up, pausing a step away, and murmured, "Sir. Ferry."

Ferry beamed at him. "I was wondering... um, you said you'd met Lord Carillon. Rufus Pride."

Carillon nodded at Rufus. "Afternoon." Amiable, but with more distance than their first meeting.

"Sir." Rufus made a slight bow. "A pleasant day today."

Carillon considered. "Rather, yes. And not raining. Though I gather from some of the gossip we could use more. I'm still getting used to thinking of the weather that way."

He was so comfortable in his skin. Rufus couldn't bear it for a moment, like everything went his way, would always go his way. That the weather was no great thing, a conversation to have, rather than harm or salvation.

Ferry shifted in her seat. "What way, sir?"

Carillon waved a hand, contemplating. "I'm used to how the weather affects travel, of course. Too much rain and the roads bog down. Too little, and you breathe dust for weeks. Too dry and there's a tremendous risk of fire, some places. In others, there's ice and snow, and you can't get across some mountain passes or bridges for months at a time."

He looked out at the green, and the people there. "This is different. Weather makes the crops grow, or decides what happens to the ponies or the deer or the trees or the plants. And I don't know much about that. Yet."

Rufus was quiet for a minute. "Haven't lived here for a long time." It wasn't a question, it was far too grudging for that.

Carillon shook his head. "I was at school from the time I was thirteen. A preparatory tutoring school during the week from when I was eleven. A little one, in someone's house, but still. Not here. That was in Cornwall," he added to Ferry. "Apprenticeship, a less formal one than some, but that was travelling. And then I was travelling or there was the War. I've been back for a week or a month here or there in all seasons, but not living through them, the slow changes."

Rufus had no idea what to make of this. A moment later, Ferry explained, gently, "It's common for people in the First Families to go to school to get ready to go to school. A little silly, but there you are. More structured than a private governess or tutor, more interaction with other people. Build relationships. Sometimes it's with the family you will apprentice with, later. To get to know them. Sometimes it's oh, five, maybe ten students at a time. Enough to build connections, not really a formal school."

Carillon nodded and then made a face. "Only two of us from those two years made it through the War. As it turns out." He stopped, then said, "But the idea was sound."

Rufus nodded, not sure how to identify the emotion he could hear in Carillon's voice, under the surface. There was an awkward long pause, then Rufus asked, "Are you finding out what you want to know in the village, then?"

There was a minute pause, and Carillon said "Some of it, yes. I'm still trying to decide about hiring for positions on the estate. I want to take my time and do it right. The right skills, but also the right personality. I've always thought a good staff had to fit in together. Complement each other." And then he added, "Trying to figure out who's trustworthy."

"Sir?" Rufus was curious about that, enough to risk asking.

"Oh, I've heard the rumours about smuggling. And I certainly know it's had a long history here, but I also know enough to know there're different kinds of smuggling. It's one thing to dodge taxes - not ideal, mind you, but one understands why people might. But it's another to destroy things, animals, communities, in the process. Or hurt people unnecessarily."

Rufus looked up sharply, but Carillon was watching him, smooth and calm and not giving anything away. He almost opened his mouth to ask why Carillon cared if people got hurt, and he couldn't figure out how to say it.

Ferry made a noise. "Does that really go on, Lord Carillon? I mean, I'd think - I'd think maybe it wasn't so necessary anymore?" Rufus couldn't help looking at her, at how innocent she was of the things that went on in the Forest, what needed to go on.

Carillon shrugged. "The need for money goes on, even when the world changes. And some people like the risk and challenge, even without the money. And most people like a bit of luxury."

He kept himself pointed toward Rufus, and Rufus couldn't figure out if he knew or guessed or just was aimed that way. He couldn't say anything, or he would give it away.

Ferry was still puzzled, her attention flicking back and forth between the two, before she said, "Oh." She sounded a little defeated. "Even though it hurts people? And animals? What kinds of things do they smuggle?"

Rufus couldn't answer this, he knew he couldn't, and after another too-long pause, Carillon said, "I've heard rumours of different things. Rare flowers. Rare animals, for private collections or their parts. You know, you must have read, how many of them go into devices or inks or a potion or salve. Magically grown woods, taken from the people who've invested years in the growing."

Ferry made another noise, this one less bewildered. "Oh, like the yew. That's why it's part of the common rights."

Rufus nodded, at least he could do that much.

Carillon watched her, steadily, then he said, "I should have you up to Ytene, Ferry, sometime. Show you around a bit."

She lit up at that, the distraction clearly worked. "Oh, would you? I'd like that very much if it wouldn't impose. I understand you've a grand hall there, and some - was it mosaics? And I heard you have some tapestries?"

Carillon nodded. "Mosaics. They hold their colour quite well, really. Replicas of some Roman ones in the family properties way back, and then a set along the walls and ceiling in the same general style. The tapestries, though, they need a fair bit of work. Quite faded, I'm sad to say."

Ferry asked several more questions about that, before saying "I got asked if you'd be hiring from the town." Which made Carillon put his hands up with a laughing, "I beg mercy, my lady. I'm still sorting out what's needed." And then they got into a discussion of what a great house needed, and Ferry recommending a few people. People she'd been talking to, in some detail.

Rufus felt increasingly left out, retreating a little in body, crossing his arms across his chest. She took several minutes to notice, and then she said, quietly, "Oh, sorry, Rufus."

And then, more daringly, she declared "Lord Carillon, this has been very pleasant, but I'd made arrangements for Rufus to walk me back. I know he's got other things in his evening. And I really ought to get back to give Nanny a little break before the children go to bed."

Carillon stood promptly. "Of course, dear lady. I'd not dream of keeping you. I do hope we can find a time for you to come to Ytene soon. Will you send a note round and let me know a convenient afternoon or two for you?"

Ferry nodded. "Of course. I'll send one tonight."

Rufus made a small noise, and she said, "There are the magical journals. Still very new." They were not cheap, Rufus knew, but very efficient. Like so many magical things, really.

Carillon stood, bowed, and extracted a small card case from his jacket. "Here are my details, for that." Ferry smiled and rummaged in her own bag to offer him one of her cards. And then there was the bowing and smiling and formal leave-taking until finally Rufus could nod and step away with her.

He didn't know what to do with his hands. She didn't reach out to take his arm or his hand, so they walked off, to the road back to Boar Court, silent, stiff, uncomfortable.

SIXTEEN

NEAR BOAR COURT

Rufus and Ferry were well down the road before either of them spoke, and then they both spoke together, a jumble of words. Rufus gestured at her. "Please."

Ferry swallowed, then said, very cautious, "Something went wrong there, didn't it? But I don't know what." She wasn't sure what to do except to ask.

Rufus was silent, down the road, past the marker to other villages, other kinds of lives. Ferry watched him, closely.

"I didn't expect to see you with him," he said, finally.

Ferry wasn't sure what to make of his tone, and so it was several more steps before she said, "Did you think..." She stopped. "Did you think he was courting me?"

Put that bluntly, it at least got an answer "Yes. No. Maybe. I don't - I - was he?"

Ferry stopped and put her hands on her hips. "Honestly, Rufus." She was somewhere between amused and offended. "Did you think I was that easy-hearted?"

Rufus had to stop too, and then he looked down and away, not sure what to say.

"Hey." She reached out to touch his chin, nudge it upwards with a finger. "Hey."

He looked up - he couldn't not - and she was watching him intently. She felt suddenly much older than she was, or more experienced. But something in this clearly upset Rufus even more, because he took a step back, twisting to look down and away.

Ferry watched for a moment, then said, "Rufus, don't go, please."

He nearly spun at that, part of him visibly wanting to run and be anywhere else than here. But she was asking, and so he took a breath, and another, and took a step back, but steadied himself.

"He could give you all the things you deserve," Rufus said. It came out sullen and grudging to her ear.

"Oh, good grief." She wasn't sure what to say to this, and that was probably not the useful thing, but it came out of her mouth anyway. "Honestly, Rufus. About the fourth thing, he said to me. This was after making sure my family was the one he thought and asking about the children and their parents. Anyway, he asked if my family hoped he'd take an interest, and pointed out I was far too young for him."

Rufus rocked back on his heels. "Too... young?" That was clearly not what he'd expected.

"He's near forty. Or over. I didn't actually inquire, I could look it up if you're curious when I get home."

"Look it up?" He sounded like a broken mimic bird.

Ferry let out a puff of breath. "There're books. Of the family connections, and lists when people were born. I was decent at maths, and that's just subtraction." The fact she was babbling was, really, not a great sign.

Rufus was back on the age. "Too young?"

Ferry nodded. "He's right. He's fifteen years older, give or take. I pointed out my parents wanted me to marry someone who's fifty, nearly sixty. He was outraged at who that was, so we rather got onto a different topic."

"Outraged?" Rufus was only managing brief exclamations and echoes, increasingly agitated.

"Apparently he's got a horrid reputation? Lord Carillon offered to see if he could put a word in my family's ears this summer. Some reasons they'd take seriously about why he'd be a bad match. Like him being on shaky ground with money."

Something in that sentence went over very badly. Ferry could see it in the way Rufus stiffened up. But he shook his head and stayed quiet.

"Rufus? You're worrying me."

There was a long pause - all she could do was let the silence draw out. Finally, he said, carefully, "It's hard. Watching people who have so much."

She made a small noise and then said. "Look. Can we find somewhere to sit down? Talk a little? Not... do this in the middle of the road?"

Rufus nodded. "A little further on. There's a meadow." They walked in silence, down the road for a quarter mile, until he pointed off at a path to a meadow, sheltered from the road by trees. He helped her over a few fallen logs, holding her hand just long enough for balance while she managed her skirts. At last they found a piece of dry ground to sit on.

"Talk to me, please?" she said finally.

He was quiet for another minute, then said "It's hard for me to see people who have things. When I don't. And - Lord Carillon could buy the village, several times over. Every store, every worker, every... everything."

Ferry made a noise. "All right. Yes. I suppose."

"Your books don't tell you how much money he makes?" That came out very bitter and sharp, and she flinched away.

"Not in numbers like that," she admitted.

"He could, oh, save the bookshop. You know how Mrs Gates worries about money. He could mend dozens of cottages, so people didn't worry about dying of coughs in the winter. He could mend the roads, so people didn't lose stock and carriages in the mud. Set up a portal here rather than people having to go down to Beaulieu or up to Salisbury Minor. Bring in a Healer, here, in the village, full time, instead of sharing between half a dozen villages, never there when you need them." That, oh, that broke him open.

Ferry made a distressed sound, but it seemed like he barely heard her. He was off, now, in a world of his own, miserable and trapped. "That's what did for my parents. If someone had seen them the first day they were sick, good chance they'd be alive now. Good chance. But we'd only the one Healer, wasn't her day to be up here, didn't get here until - until after they were dead and buried. Fresh dirt on the grave."

Ferry could barely breathe, and she reached out, cautiously, to touch his hand. He jerked his hand away, pushing hers back. "Don't." It was sharp and hard. But she couldn't leave him. Not like this.

"I've got a cottage, coming down around my ears, and no prospects. He sits there and has money and looks comfortable, not worrying where his next meal's coming from. And I helped him, on the road, he gave me coin for it, but that's a week's food, if I'm careful, and I'm almost out. Does he offer me a job? Even suggest I come see if there's something might suit? He doesn't. Doesn't even ask. Doesn't hire from the village where the coin might get spread around. Only two, so far. Two! That estate should have two dozen even if they're running scant and the lord's away."

It was turning into a river, now, a flood of words, pouring out like acid, before he started to repeat himself. He kept coming back to the coin and the money and the fears that kept him awake at night.

He took a long time to run down into silence, and pull back, away from her. She waited until he was quiet, then said, "That's been building a while, eh?"

It was the dryness of her voice, and the gentleness, that he'd had a fit of temper. But that it had lanced something, her recognition, like his mother, and it snapped his head up. He was wide-eyed, unsteady, but he nodded.

"He's a pleasant man, Rufus." Ferry was clear. "But he's not the man I want to be in a meadow with. Like this, or like we were, either of them."

He blinked again, not making sense of this.

"Mind." Her voice turned considering. "I will have more of a word, when I visit, about one's obligation to the local village. I'll see if he can't step up hiring a bit, even if it some of it's temporary. I'm sure there're things to clean out in the house, dusting and polishing. Or wood to be cleared from the grounds, or such."

He ventured, "Do you know about houses like that, then?"

She nodded. "I'm expected to marry the kind of family has a house like that. Well, something like that. Ytene's something special, I gather. But big, with a staff of dozens."

Rufus drew back a little. "You're not like me."

Ferry let out a long breath. "We come from very different places. And I don't." She stopped, then tried that again. "I don't know the fears you've lived with. For years. Like that. But I know they're real. They matter. And maybe we can figure out some things. Together. Maybe I'll see something you don't. Different perspective. Experience. And maybe you'll see something that helps me. I mean, besides the parts you've already done." That brought a blush back to her cheeks.

It made him smile, and he said, "Well, then." And then a quiet, "Ought to get you back. Sun's getting lower."

Ferry nodded, and then she ventured, "Do you know people who are smuggling?"

He sucked in a breath. "Got a good guess who some of them might be. Nothing solid I could take to the Guard. It's." He tried to figure out a way that wouldn't hit his oath. "Like Lord Carillon said. Long tradition here. The same families, generation to generation, often. It's not knowing who's doing it, it's catching them doing it that's the trick."

She shook her head. "I don't like the idea of people - or plants or animals - getting hurt."

Rufus pushed himself standing, suddenly. "Like or not, not always a thing in our power to fix." He held out a hand to her, and she took it, let him pull her up. "I'll walk you home."

It was very final, as an end to the conversation, and they walked back to the end of the drive to the Court in silence.

SEVENTEEN

TRUE EYEWORTH

I t was Monday afternoon, and Rufus had come through the village, looking for a few odd jobs. Still no luck. He felt, more than saw, two people come up, one on either side.

"Johnny." He glanced at his other side. "Will." It was not wise to make Will upset. He had a mighty fist and a short temper. And he normally did what Johnny told him.

"Saw you on the road, we did."

"Did you, Johnny?"

"Walking your lady friend back."

Rufus shrugged. "Man can do that, can't he?"

Johnny laughed, clapping him on the shoulder. "Man can dream. She's not in your league, Rufus, boy."

Rufus glanced over,. "Why d'you say that?"

Johnny gestured at Will, and Will grunted. "Saw her." His voice was rough. "Talking Lord Carillon. She's aiming far above your head, laddie."

Rufus looked away, feeling that burst of jealousy take hold again, clench at his heart. All around the edges, smooth as a snake, there was Johnny's voice. "Course, you helping with our little job might be a thing. Plenty of money to buy the lady pretty things. A house, not a cottage. A pony of her own and a cart to drive around in."

It was impossible to know what to say, other than "Already said I'm in, Johnny. You don't need to ask again."

"Ah, but are you all in?"

"What do you mean by that, Johnny?"

"Not sure about you at all, boy. You and your queer ways." Johnny was speculative.

Rufus let out a puff of breath. "Johnny, glad to answer questions. You want steady land, I can do that, you know that. Used to…"

Used to with Johnny's son. Before the war. When Rufus came back and Peter didn't.

Johnny shrugged, quiet. "Want your word you won't tell anyone. On your magic and your ma's grave. No word, no hint, no nothing."

"She asked, Johnny, if I knew about the people smuggling."

Johnny was sharp - and Rufus could suddenly feel a dagger against his back just below the rib. "And what did you say to that, then?"

Rufus swallowed, then said. "Said I could guess at some of them. Didn't say I knew any for sure. Nothing I could take to the Guard. You've not done a thing wrong, by the law. Just asked me to. Said it was a long tradition here, that it wasn't knowing who, it was catching them doing it was the trick. Already promised you I'd not share the details. Lead anyone there."

Johnny considered, and Rufus could feel the point of the dagger slowly recede. "Well, then. Mind you keep it that way. And you didn't say a word to that high and mighty lord?"

"No, Johnny. Hoping I could go to him for work, clearing the estate. He'd not want to hire me if he knew."

Too late, he realised he'd given Johnny an excellent hold over him, the threat of letting his name get around as associated with smuggling.

Johnny was smug when he spoke again. "Well, then. That's a thing to know." Then his voice turned sharper. "Your lady light know about your war?"

"A little. Not had a lot of time together."

"And not all of it talking, then? Know you've had a few hours if you'd wanted talk."

Rufus jerked for a moment, the implications of how closely they'd been keeping an eye on him. "A few," he said grudgingly.

Johnny grunted. "So." He continued walking in silence for several strides. "You're in. You won't say a word. Even if his Lordship asks. Or it won't go well for you."

"Been clear, Johnny."

They walked, making another half-loop of the green, before Johnny said, "Had someone ask if you could handle the ground, for sure."

Rufus shrugged. "Done it here or there, for ages. Bigger bog, bit more effort. I'll go first if you want."

Will grunted. "Could lead us wrong."

It took a good bit of self-control. "Last thing I'd do is lead someone into being..." He had to stop and shiver. "Buried alive."

Johnny twisted, peering at him. "Sincere enough. Let him be, Will."

That wasn't the end of it though. Johnny coughed, and said, "So, we'll be wanting some things from you, besides the bogs."

Rufus glanced sideways. "Sure, Johnny. Said I was in. What sort of thing?"

"Got an offer for a special sort of cargo. Might want to see what you can do about - you had that trick with the invisible wall, right?"

Rufus frowned. "Something you want to keep out, or something you want to keep in?"

"Keep out," Johnny said. "Well, away. Other side of a wall."

"Possibly," Rufus said. "Depends on - how big. The wall, I mean."

"Thought you were this great magician, strongest out of the villages in an age."

"It's not like that, Johnny. Don't know how to use a lot of it."

"Wasn't that what you were learning?"

"Learning, Johnny. Only had two years with Master Burleigh."

"Two years is plenty." Johnny was dismissive. "No time for modesty, boy, we've big plans afoot." He made a discontented noise. "So, what can you do then? And for how long?"

Rufus let out a long breath and thought hard. Clearly, whatever he said was important, and they'd expect him to do it.

"Come on, boy." Johnny was growing impatient.

"Master Burleigh taught me some of the charms. The old ones. Worked out a few since. Mostly, can affect - natural things. Manmade, not so much. It's why I can't fix my roof. Manmade is harder. More complicated. And we didn't have time to get to the complicated."

Johnny cuffed him on the shoulder. "Man up. No excuses. What can you do, and what can't you?"

Rufus swallowed. "Steady a bog. Take maybe ten loaded ponies at a time, and men to lead them. Need to be there, focusing on it, while they cross, line of sight." Which varied a lot in the forest. Depending on the bog.

Johnny sounded approving and then demanded "What else?"

"Wall - taller, and I can't go so far to the sides. Further out, and it's only 'bout three feet high. Line of sight again." There were ways to do things out of sight, but he hadn't learned those.

That got a grunt. "You had a knack for the wild things."

"Can calm some of them. Family knack for the horses though I'm not so good as Da and Jasper were. Didn't learn that either." He paused, trying to figure out a way out of the next problem. There was a thing he didn't want to tell Johnny, but he was pretty sure Johnny remembered. If he didn't tell, there'd be trouble.

"Boy?"

Rufus coughed, then said "Can usually tell where there're animals. Anything breathes. Have to concentrate on it, can't do other magics while I am." Also a skill he hadn't had time to learn, doing more than one thing at once.

That got a pleased sound. "Remember you and the adder." And Peter. Who they never talked about.

Rufus nodded slightly.

"What's your range on that? And can you tell what they are, then, or just that there's things?"

"About how big they are. Know what deer are like, and pigs and ponies and sheep."

Johnny nodded. "We'll be wanting that. You practice up or make up what you need for it. Might need you to help us a track a specific thing. We know more or less where it's like to be, but will need to close in on it."

"Can tell you what's in that direction, Johnny, yeah, a good quarter mile out if there's no hill in between."

"You've heard the stories about the white hart? We've a request for one, high price for taking it alive. You'll be helping with that. We'll be wanting your other skills, too." And then "Can you make lights?"

Rufus shook his head. "No." Some people, he knew, could flick their fingers, have a ball of cool-burning light in their hand, easy as breathing, like Lord Carillon. Not him.

Johnny nodded. "Make things lighter?"

"No, Johnny. Most of that's manmade, yeah? Not so good with that." Good to remind him of the categories. Try to, anyway.

"Well. That's a thing." Johnny shook out his hand like he'd been angling for a bit of something fierce and the moment was gone. "You practice up. All of those. Get whatever you need to do them."

"Don't need much." Fortunately. It's not like Johnny was offering money for components. Some magics needed them, a thing you shifted to change the world. His just ran on pure mental insistence. The ones he knew.

"You keep your mouth shut, then. May have a need for you, a day or two before the big day. I'll let you know."

They walked another round in near silence, barring Johnny murmuring a thing or two about other people in the village. Who owed him a favour. Who kept their eyes open. There was a point to that, Rufus was sure, but he couldn't figure it out at the moment.

EIGHTEEN

TRUE EYEWORTH

They sent Ferry out to the village on Monday, to fetch the Healer for Nanny, whose cold was not improving. It took a few minutes to track her down and arrange to drive her back to the house when she was done seeing people waiting for her in the village. An hour or so.

Ferry caught sight of Rufus, by the green. She was about to call out or go over to him, or something, and then she saw two men come up, one on either side of him. Ferry pulled back into a narrow alley between two houses, and watched them go around, speaking in low voices she couldn't overhear. She didn't like the way they were. Hard and sharp and dangerous, somehow, though they weren't doing anything obviously threatening.

When they were walking away from her, wouldn't see her, she slipped out of the alley and made her way down to the bookshop, pushing the door open. "Hey, Pross?"

There was another customer, just finishing, and so Ferry waited, shifting from foot to foot with some impatience until the door closed. She waited until Pross waved her on. "Before you burst." Her voice was dry. "What are you up to, Ferry?"

"Can you see the men with Rufus, Pross? Out the window? On that side?"

Pross let out a sigh, and went over to look out the window that faced the square before she said, "That's Johnny and Will."

"Why don't I know them?"

"Because they're not very nice men, and they go to the pub, drink a lot, make deals, and go home and drink more." Pross's voice was clipped. "You don't want to be doing anything with the likes of them."

"Then why're they talking to Rufus?"

Pross winced. "I've a few guesses, none I like very much. They're..." She paused, and then rummaged for something in her desk, tapping it, and it lit up, three times, in a glowing blue. "All right, no one's overhearing. They're - well, gossip says, they're smugglers. Very active ones. Not just the people who do it once or twice, or only occasional. In deep."

"So why are they talking to Rufus?" Ferry could hear her voice getting higher and more anxious and tight.

"You should ask him." Pross was abrupt.

Ferry winced, and said, "Mind if I get tea?" Pross shook her head. "Take your time."

"Got to drive Healer Edwards over to Nanny, when she's done seeing people. Her cough's still bad. That's why I came to town."

Pross grimaced. "I'll let you know if I see her come out, then."

Ferry nodded, and went upstairs to the flat, putting the kettle on. It was just boiling, when she heard the door open again, the front of the store and someone come in. She had her tea, fairly quickly, and edged down the stairs, not trying to be quiet, but avoiding the creaky board on the fourth step out of habit.

Through the door, she heard, "Look, you've just said you've an idea what they're up to."

"Knowing people might be - free traders - is different from knowing a specific thing they're after. And I don't know what they're after, and I don't want them after me." Pross's voice was fierce by the end.

It was quiet for a little, and Ferry almost opened the door. But then she heard the other voice. She could tell it was male, now, a tenor rather than something lower. He went on, "I need something I can take to a magistrate."

"Not going to come from me, sir. They don't tell me that kind of thing."

"Why not?" The voice was now curious, not pressing as hard.

Ferry could hear her friend's shrug in the mix of distaste and bitterness. "Because I'm not from here. Because I'm a woman. Because my husband wasn't one of them. Any of those would be reason enough."

"Surely they've used women in the past?"

"Oh, you've heard that old tale, about Lovey Warne, wrapping the silks and lace around her body, putting her dress on again, and riding off? Might have been true then. Not so true now. Hasn't been for a while." A little shrug. "Or rather, if they do, the women are a lot subtler about it than the men. Now, that I'd believe."

There was a hollow laugh. "So. When they're not promenading around the green, where would I find them?"

"The Wheel," Pross said, naming the pub. "But they'll not talk when there are strangers about. Especially strangers like you."

The man let out a long sigh. "Live in the Forest for centuries, still an in-comer."

Pross snorted. "It's not the time, it's the class."

The man murmured something Ferry couldn't hear, and then, "Can't fix the stars we were born under. Should I go lurk round the pub anyway, do you think?"

"You're going to do it whether or not I think it would be a good idea, so why don't you go do that?"

That got another hollow laugh from him. "Come on, Proserpina, I've known you since you were thirteen and in double braids, in awe of the Owlery. Give a man a little more than that?"

Pross was quiet for a bit, and then she said, "Geoffrey, I'm not as brave as I was back then, nor as sharp. They're luxuries I can't afford."

He made a small apologetic noise, and then a "We're neither of us the people we were then, are we? I think you're near the only person left who calls me Geoffrey, not Carillon or Lord Carillon or some such."

Ferry rocked back on her heels for a moment and missed the next murmur from Pross. She caught the end, a "... think about it, come back in a day or two. Buy a book while you're at it."

This got a sound out of him, and a "I will bring a list, how's that? Do take care, Proserpina, and my best to Cammie." There were the sounds of the door opening and closing, shifting and moving.

Ferry waited another minute or two, tried to figure out if she could fake the sound of coming downstairs. She stepped up two steps silently and came down them loudly, and then pushed the door to the private spaces open. "Sorry I took a bit."

It was not clear to her if she'd fooled Pross - Pross rarely gave that kind of thing away.

Pross was polishing an already spotless bit of wood and started when Ferry came to the front of the store. "Oh, sorry, I was - "

Ferry shook her head. "I shouldn't keep you. I should get back and see about Healer Edwards."

Pross looked like she wanted to argue, or say something, but she shook her head. "Tell Nanny I hope she feels better. And oh, take her this? I offered to order it, she can send round the payment next time someone comes to town."

"You sure?"

"Your credit's good, and hers. Other people's, not so much."

It seemed a sideways commentary on the earlier conversation, not that Ferry could ask about that at all. She nodded and ducked out the door to find the Healer, the pony cart, and the road back to Boar Court, in that order.

NINETEEN

TRUE EYEWORTH

They permitted Rufus to escape the direct attentions of Johnny and Will after one final reminder of where his loyalties ought to lie. It involved a sharp elbow to his ribs, enough to ache for three days, he reckoned. Not long enough to limit him in the job itself.

They had told him to make his way back to the pub in about half an hour, to sit and listen and learn. Which meant money for drinks, his own at least, and he really didn't have it.

The alternative was to go back to a leaking cottage and no light outside the fireplace, and less company, and that was also not at all appealing. Besides the fact it would make Johnny angry. So to the pub it was.

He was most of the way there, walking from the bench where he'd sat down after the elbow, when he caught an odd movement near the pub and inn. Something that wasn't there but there enough to notice. Something that felt a little queer, a little twisted in the world.

Rufus blinked at it several times, trying to get his eyes to focus. Then he saw it, a transparent outline of a man, if he looked away and then back. Just a flicker. So easy to over-look and ignore. He could see why no one else was noticing.

On the one hand, the man was listening at the pub. Where there were smugglers plotting. On the other hand, who was Rufus to do something about that? He couldn't do much himself without violence. He could tell Johnny, which was violence. And the man was out in the alley, not sneaking up on someone. Just listening at the window, to a conversation anyone could hear if they stood at just the right angle.

It occurred to Rufus for the first time that maybe Johnny didn't know about that corner. They cracked the window sometimes, to let a little fresh air in among the pipe smoke and the beer fumes. When they did, something odd happened with the sound, and it echoed to a particular spot in the alley.

Johnny was never the one standing outside, wanting to be inside. Johnny was in the centre of things. Always had been. It made Rufus stop in his tracks, trying to wrestle with the cascade of thoughts.

Rufus had always been on the outside. Youngest of his brothers, and by enough he wasn't able to keep up with them when he was younger. Before they went, one by one, to war, without him.

He'd been cleverer than most in school. Not clever enough to pass the exams for Schola, there had been ques-tions he couldn't begin to answer, about things he'd never ever heard of. But much more than the average at the village schools.

He liked reading; the teacher lent him books. He liked being outside, watching the animals; they encouraged him to keep observation notebooks. And he loved the ponies, figuring out what made each of their little herd happiest, how they liked to have things done, treating them like the individual queens they were.

People, though. People were so tricky. He'd liked Peter. They'd been nearly of an age. Back then, Johnny hadn't been so hard and sharp.They'd come from different places, for all they lived in the same region of the Forest. Johnny smuggled, and made deals, and had money.

Rufus's father worked hard, repairing things, patching together repairs for whoever needed it. Magical and not, depending who had work, moving between the worlds. Non-magical folk didn't need to know he used magic to make the new pieces or hold a repair in place. The Silence didn't care about that, a thing they could never figure out. It had been a living, even after he wasn't in with the smugglers anymore.

And if Johnny had done better over time, well, no one minded too much. Most smuggling helped the villages, it didn't hurt them. It took things they had in plenty and traded them for things they didn't have. Rum. Tea. Good hard coin. Connections, sometimes. The things city folks took for granted, they said.

So. Johnny didn't have much experience with standing outside the pub, wondering what they were talking about inside. All the little give and take, that made someone likely to hire a friend more than someone they didn't know. Or just the outright giving work to their friends.

Rufus thought through what he'd promised. He wasn't obligated to tell Johnny about things that might threaten his plans. He didn't even really know Johnny's plans, other than the parts he could guess at from the questions just now. Ergo, he wasn't obligated to protect Johnny. Just to not tell what was in that first conversation.

Wait. Johnny hadn't made him promise anything else.

Not for this conversation. So what did that mean? He couldn't assume Johnny had forgotten, so that meant some other reason, more terrifying than a slip of the mind. Johnny had started to say something, there had been the dagger, and yet there was no further demanded promise.

He thought through the options, paying close attention for when the oath-magic closed around him and pulled in tighter. Couldn't go tell someone Johnny was smuggling. Not that that was news to anyone.

Could tell someone that he knew someone smuggling, who'd asked about specific magics. But that wasn't evidence would hold up in court. He'd named no specific animals besides the white hart, and that was rare but he didn't think it was restricted. No specific other people, other than Will and Bolton, whose names he couldn't give. A promise of a lot of money, but not where it was coming from.

Rufus let out a puff of breath. All right, then. He'd go in and listen, see if he could figure out more of the details. And worry over why Johnny hadn't asked for a broader oath. Or what he'd expect when he did.

The inn was about two thirds full - people were still out at work, many of them. He sidled up to the bar to order a half-pint, and Johnny caught sight of him, and called out "Put his drinks on my tab today." Rufus looked up, startled, caught entirely off balance. That was a public declaration of connection, far more than he'd expected.

Thomas, the publican, tilted his head. "Pint of bitter, please." The cheapest local brew - more than he got normally, but not taking any advantage of Johnny's generosity.

Rufus waited until it was poured, then came over and Johnny waved him at a bench. Out of the immediate close circle, but close enough he could hear a bit of it. He ended up next to two older men, who nodded and went back to their low-voiced long-standing argument about racing. Rufus was not sure if they meant racing ponies or hedgehogs or ferrets.

As he sat, he kept hearing little snippets of the conversation. This person was working on something that sounded like a cage. Another repairing a decent sized... not a cart, some sedan chair contraption, designed to be carried on the shoulders by several men. Someone else putting together salves against poison.

"Boy, do you know much about recipes?" It was another older man, too old to do a smuggling run, but whose planning was still respected. Jack.

Rufus looked up sharply. "Not too much. Mum knew a lot more."

That gets a considering, then a "You have her Book?" The book she kept all her personal recipes in.

Rufus went still, a mouse trying to avoid the hawk above him, then said "Kept in shorthand. Know a little, but not enough I'd trust anything without lots of testing." He'd trust the runes if he could make them work, but she'd only written down sketches of those, no precautions or notes. Those had lived in her head, and they were lost now.

"Shame. Her people always had a nice line in cures. Lots of things they didn't share." The end of the sentence turned hard. "That was unfriendly, like."

Rufus swallowed. "Mum had her ways." It was mildly said, and he felt Jack considering him.

"And what are your ways, then?"

Rufus glanced at Johnny, who was clearly paying attention. "Trying to keep body and magic t'gether, sir," he said. "Taking work where I can find it. Didn't get a chance to learn a lot of skills. Good at digging a trench and shoring it up, but don't want to be in one ever again."

The last was a risk, but it sometimes helped.

Jack made a dismissive noise. "No trade?"

"Was supposed to be learning magic. No one to teach, now. Master Burleigh's gone. And Mistress Donne died two winters gone."

She'd been ancient when he was still in short trousers, well over a hundred and twenty. She'd not have been a good teacher for him, they'd known that the first they met, but she'd given him a few hints. "And there's Master Donovan, but he does ships and I've no sea legs."

He wanted land. Solid land and trees above him, and ponies and deer and pigs and sheep in the background.

"Didn't I see, in the paper. Oy, Dick. Got the paper there, yesterday's?"

The publican nodded, and a paper was ceremoniously passed over, person by person. Jack unfolded it, peered at it. It was the gaze of someone who didn't care much for reading but did it because sometimes people didn't tell you things any other way.

"Here, boy." He folded the paper back and tapped an article. Rufus read. "Looking for likely men and women for magical training." Someone who wanted to train people who'd come of age during the war, who didn't have the skills they might have without the war.

Rufus looked up. "Sir." He was careful. "Sounds like I'd have to go to Trellech." Wales. Decidedly not the Forest.

"That a problem, boy? You could come back after."

Come back to a broken down hut, to ponies who'd had no care. More spaces that were ghosts and hollow and wrong. If he did that, he could never come back, and that would kill him. Slow, but sure.

Jack waved a hand. "But we need people know what they're doing. The magics. The complicated ones."

Rufus ducked his chin. "I'll think on it, sir. Thank you for telling me." Even if it made Rufus uncomfortable, just the thought.

Fortunately, then someone else came in, and Johnny was all good cheer, and ordering drinks all round. Rufus got pressed into service to deliver them, being the junior among them by a lot.

TWENTY

Thursday, Rufus brought a note round and left it with the staff, asking if she'd be free on her half day. She stared at it for a good twenty minutes, sitting in the library where the children were working on lessons. Until Caelus came and leaned on her shoulder to try and read it.

It was not badly written, really. Oh, his handwriting was curious in places, not the proper angles she'd been taught, but it was neat and tidy and quite individual.

Ferry,

If you are free on Thursday afternoon, I would like to see you and ask you about something. I am afraid I cannot offer a picnic, just company. If you agree, I will be down in the clearing from last week.

Sincerely,
Rufus

Plainspoken, clearly giving her the choice. He'd be

waiting in the meadow, rather than at the bottom of the drive, so if she chose not to come, she'd not have to see him.

Ferry shook her head and said to her pupils "I'll be upstairs for a few minutes. You finish working on your Latin translation, both of you, and I'll be down by the time you're finishing." Upstairs, she changed into her favourite green dress and found the green and blue scarf that went well with it. Then it was down to the kitchen to ask Cook if she might put together a generous basket for her.

An hour later, the children were occupied with a project that could be supervised by a housemaid and keep them out of Nanny's hair. Ferry set out with the basket over her arm, walking down to the meadow. She'd been very vague about when to expect her back, with Cook and Nanny and the maid, but no one was expecting her until dark.

When she came through the path, she saw the pony, and called out "Hey, Star." Then there was Rufus, who had clearly been waiting nervously for her. He immediately held out a hand to take the basket then his other to her, and she slipped her fingers into his.

"I wasn't sure..."

"I'd have written before, but I didn't know where." Ferry was apologetic.

Rufus turned bright red, which she found very endearing. "Oh. Um. Sorry. Yeah."

She smiled and shifted to stand on tiptoe and kiss his cheek. "So I'm here. Cook made a picnic. I wasn't sure what you'd like, and I couldn't really tell her I was meeting you? So it's chicken and cheese, and some scones and things."

"Oh." He had a strange expression on his face, and she turned to him, looking at him more closely. "I didn't... I didn't mean."

Ferry took a breath. "It's pretty clear you don't have much, Rufus. That's what you're trying to figure out. A few sandwiches, they're not a problem." She paused, then said, "I asked if there any jobs at the Hall. And there aren't, but they said they'd see if they knew anyone."

Rufus closed his eyes and went completely still again. "Oh."

Ferry watched him, and then said, "People know." And then a "And that's why... um. Gentlemen of the Night have been seen talking to you?"

He shuddered, and said, "Made me take an oath." He was so plaintive and uneasy, Ferry immediately nodded, drawing him down to the blankets he'd laid out. Then he swallowed and said "Let me. Let me tell what I can? Please don't ask me things?"

He took a while to say much.

"We've never had much money, my family, or training for things. But we made do. Mum did sewing for people, or a little nursing, checking in if someone was ill, nothing fancy. Not like a Healer, just - being there, making soup. Doing wash. Da made things. My brothers were learning trades. Not - like I was, like they hoped I would? But enough to keep them together, let them start families. Be a bit better off than Mum and Da."

Ferry nodded, listening intently.

Rufus was quiet, then a "When they did the testing, when I was twelve." His voice was a bit uneven. "They said I had a lot of power. There was talk about - giving me a year to learn better for the exams. There was a lot on them I didn't know. Not just the questions for Schola, but other things. But in the end, they asked Master Burleigh to take me on. He said I - could learn what I needed with him. That it might be a bit slower, but I could learn with him.

Only. Only he had to go to war. When I'd not been there two years."

"That. You must have been so lost. Two years is just - starting. Even at Schola."

Rufus nodded. "I'd learned a bit. But - only pieces. Listening to the ground. Getting a sense of where animals are. The trees. More with the horses. Very practical things." He tapped his fingers on his leg for a moment. "And then my brothers went one by one. And then I went." He looked away. "I don't want to talk about that. Not right now. Not..."

"You don't have to." That was prompt.

"I came home, invalided out, and I - I don't remember much. Not when I first got home. I was coming out of it when - the Naples Scourge. When they died." He had to stop, pausing in the rush of memory and grief.

"When they died. I got to keep the hut. The - rights, they go with the huts, the land. Not the people. So I could keep the ponies, and the pigs and the cow and the chickens. Have enough food to manage with. But there's holes in the roof. I tried to fix them, and it made things worse, and there are more, and I don't dare try again. Lost the cow last year. Most of the pigs. The chickens this winter. Everything I touch turns to mud."

Ferry squeezed his hand. "Mending things is really hard." She said. "With magic, I mean. It's a whole special kind of magic, to make a thing whole again when it's worn out. Lots and lots of people can't do it. I - sort of can? I haven't done lots of different kinds of things. My teachers said that's one of the things a delicate touch is good for, so they taught me the basics. What's your cottage made of?"

Her voice was so soothing he answered her without thinking. "It's cobb. Sort of mud plaster. And thatch on the top, I got new thatch, but it didn't go together right, and it..."

His voice trailed off. "It leaks and I can't make it stop." And it was such an emblem of all that had gone wrong with his life in so many ways.

"I can look sometime. If you'd let me?" She was so cautious, now.

He nodded, shakily, and settled against her a bit more. "Money would help. Money doesn't ever not help, you know? I could fix a lot of things. So..." He tried to figure out how to phrase this.

"Um. If I were telling you a story, and said that at this bit, that's where someone comes along, and offers me a job that'd make a lot of money. The kind that'd let me fix the cottage and maybe buy a couple more mares and focus on training them, build a business like that. Breathing room. Not enough money for the rest of my life, but enough I could... have a rest of my life to look forward to. Get me out of a hole so deep I can't see a way out."

Ferry swallowed. And then carefully, she asked, "And in this story, what... kinds of things would someone need to be doing?"

Rufus shook his head. "The one thing that was specified, in the story." That felt all right, talking about it that way. "The one thing was ... I'd been learning how to make the land steady, in bogs. It's really useful," he added, defensively. "Especially here. There's patches of bogs all through the Forest."

"Not doubting the bogs." Ferry was clear about this. "The stable hands were really clear about what to look for. And how dangerous they are. They want to know which way I'm going if I'm walking by myself. Just in case, so that if I don't come back, there's a chance they could find me."

Rufus nodded. "So steadying the bog, that's a really useful skill. But it means they're planning on taking a route that would need it. With things they'd not want to take by other routes. And that's worrisome."

"Besides - setting the smuggling aside, for a moment. What's the thing you worry about? I mean, smuggling's illegal. And maybe dangerous."

"Danger. What they'd do if I didn't do what they want. How they want it. But there's more than that." He paused, gathering his thoughts.

"There's a... the Forest has opinions. You'll think I'm proper mad, but I swear it's true. There's stories, about what happens if you take the last of something, or... something the Forest doesn't want you to take. The Forest doesn't seem to mind a bit of smuggling. Ponies. Birds there's plenty of here. Plants. When there's enough for them to grow back, next season. That sort of thing. But there's stories about people who get greedy."

Ferry's voice is quiet, a little unsettled. "What happens? When the Forest is upset."

"There was someone, I was a kid, got found in a clearing. Open cages all around him, and he was - sort of mummified. All dried out. Sucked dry. It was... I didn't see it, but my brothers did."

"And they weren't telling stories?"

"About that? No. They told Mum the same thing, they were right scared."

"So you're worried that..." Her voice trailed off.

"They didn't tell me what the cargo is. Not in any detail. And yeah, I'm worried about what. The more I think about it. But I can't back out, either. Not and stay here. Going back on agreeing, that's even more dangerous."

Ferry nodded. "Can I have... a couple of minutes to think?"

He nodded. "Many as you need."

TWENTY-ONE

NEAR BOAR COURT

F erry stood and moved to walk around the clearing for a few minutes, petting Star where she was tethered each time she got near the entrance.

Rufus stayed on the blanket, watching her, not saying anything, not interrupting. Not staring. Just watching, soft-eyed, very aware of her. She circled the space five times before she came back over to the blankets with a little shake of her head. "I am trying to decide what to say, and I might as well do that with you."

He blinked up, as she settled down again, sitting rather than stretching out again. "Pardon?" he asked, finally.

"Part of me wants to be angry at you. For agreeing to do something you didn't want to do, that's dangerous and scary and also illegal." Her tone of voice made it clear the first two were, perhaps, more important.

Rufus opened his mouth, about to say something, then closed it again. "Agreed," he said, a bit careful.

"What did you actually swear?"

Rufus paused, then answered her - a bit hesitantly, she felt. "Not to tell people about the being asked." He stopped, then his voice got a bit of wonder. "The person - didn't ask for an oath on our second conversation."

"The one I saw? Around the green, Monday?"

Rufus looked up at that. "You saw that?"

"You, two men, one on either side, looking hard. Nasty."

He nodded. "Johnny was - he's the Da of one of my friends, growing up." His voice gets quiet. "Peter died in France. Fighting. Johnny wonders why it wasn't me. They all do. People liked Peter. He was - sunny. Agreeable. Bright. Not - smartest, or most power, or most skill. But the person you'd always want to work with because he'd work hard and get things done and be pleasant while he was doing it."

Ferry shifted a bit, to settle down again. "Kind of person - you'd miss a lot when he was gone."

"Like that, yeah."

"Do you think his father - resents you for that?"

"Johnny? Almost certain."

"Enough to - get you in trouble?" Ferry wasn't sure how to ask this at all.

Rufus shook his head. "I don't think so. Not like that. There aren't so many people can do much with the bogs. Bogs - take power, Master Burleigh said. Because you're affecting a big space, and you're asking it to change a lot, quite fast. And that's all about the power behind it, not - details."

Ferry chewed on her lip. "So. So. You're maybe safe for a bit?"

"Unless the Silence gets me."

"What - " Her voice was quiet. "What does it feel like to you? The Silence?"

"Like being buried alive." He shivered, despite the bright sunlight and the open meadow.

She reached out to touch his forearm, with a "Sorry."

Rufus was quiet, longer, his eyes closed, before he asked "You?"

"It feels all sharp, like a thousand pins, pressing into me. I've only once. No, twice."

"Twice?"

"Someone at school, got me to make an oath on my magic, and then..." Ferry looked away. "Some people didn't like me very much."

"What was school like for you?"

"Lots of expectations." She paused, trying to find the words for it. "Oh, there are things I liked learning. But some of our lessons were sort of - things we had to learn for later, and not always very interesting at the time. And some of them were practical things I found really hard. We lived - there are seven houses, at Schola. I was Horse. Horse is a lot kinder than most of the others, it's a thing. A value."

Rufus opened his eyes, gestured at her pendant. "Is that what it means?"

She looked down at her chest, then smiled a little. "Does. D'you want a closer look?"

He laughed. "Look at your chest? Mmm."

She blushed deeply, the colour shading down her chest to under her bodice, and a "Oh, hush, you." She then considered, and said, "We're not really supposed to take it off, but we can." She paused, then fished for the clasp on the chain, undoing the pendant.

"The green, here, that shows I was Horse. Each piece has a stone - that tells you someone's house. The setting, that tells you we were Schola. Usually silver for women, gold for men, mixed for - there are some people do both, the energies?" She set it in his hands, carefully, and he held it up, cautious like it might break. "There are other settings, for the other schools. Or for apprenticing."

"This... this is beautiful." He couldn't stop staring at it, like it was the most beautiful thing he'd seen. "Never - a gem like this."

She ducked her head. "That's an emerald. Came from my great-grandmother. She was Horse, too."

"What do the houses mean?"

"They sort us out when we first start school. Run us through different activities, exercises. Then the day school starts, when all the older students get there, they announce it, one by one. No one really knows how they choose."

"That didn't really answer? The other part?"

Ferry sucked in her breath. "People make - fun of Horses. That we're stupid. Herd animals. Prey."

"That's not nice. Horses are brave. And fierce. Some-one's never seen two stallions. Or mares protecting their herd." He sounded insulted.

That makes her smile. "Didn't make it hurt less. But each house has some things they focus on." She'd never had to explain it before. Everyone she knew what it was like even if they didn't make it to Schola. Rufus just looked at her, so patient and easygoing.

"Horse is about hard work. A lot of the house magics are things you do together, to make things flow right. They're nothing flashy, but the things that help." She pauses. "That's where I learned a bit about fixing things. It's a Horse magic, that."

"What about the others?"

She had to repeat it the way she'd learned it. "Bright is the bear, roar and protection. Bold is the boar, fierce in the fight. Charming the fox, silver-tongued beauty. Honest the horse, hard-working fellow. Knowing the owl, hidden in night. Fey is the seal, two worlds for living. Wise is the salmon, skilful in crafting."

He tilted his head. "What's white, then?"

"Owl. Why do you..." She paused, then remembered the flashing ring Lord Carillon wore. "Foxes are - a lot of them are in the Great Families. The noble ones. Not all. But a lot. Or the people who are all charming and... chatty, but figuring things out?" She wiggled a hand. "Most of my family are Owls. Learning things, but a bit mysterious about it?"

"And there are house magics?"

Ferry nods. "Pross told me one of the Fox magics - Pross's husband was a Fox, actually. She's Owl. Anyway, one of them is about keeping track of the things people tell you. Because if you're doing lots of social things, you hear different bits, and you'll have more - more - influence, if you can keep track of them."

Rufus chewed on that for a bit. "And that's the purple stones. Huh. So if I see a one of them, I should know that?"

Ferry nodded. "The house magics, not everyone learns them. Or is good at them. But it's a thing they know about. And sometimes people outside the house know about it. There's a whole set of things no one would blink twice at if I got married and taught to my husband. A few things they would, maybe." She paused, then asked, "What does Johnny wear?"

"Wear?" Rufus was startled. "Oh. You mean like - that?" He gestures at her pendant. "Or this?" He fished out the leather apprentice token, around his neck, charmed to last, but looking a bit rough around the edges. "This was what Master Burleigh gave me. Um. Nothing fancy?" And then, careful a "Copper pendant, so big, with a - I think it's an owl on it, but it's tarnished, hard to tell. On purpose, I think."

Ferry murmured, "Huh." And then a "Wonder if there's a connection. Our owls. The smugglers."

Rufus shrugged. "Why do you want to know?"

"Knowing what - someone knows. That's a kind of power. Knowing what kinds of things they might know how to do. What things they don't know how to do."

It took a bit for Rufus to sort that out. "What - kinds of things do you think he knows how to do, then?"

"Well, you know more about smuggling. What I know comes from - well, the sort of romance novels people make faces about."

Rufus had to laugh at that. "More truth in stories than people realise, sometimes. What sort of things show up there?"

"Well." Ferry had to think. "There was one about a smuggler who had a device, let him see where the Guard were. Another who had a way with the animals of the forest, to give a warning. Someone else who could make - lights, special kinds of lights. That's something we learned a little at school."

And then she shivered. "Someone who was very cruel and knew magics that made people hurt a lot. If they didn't do what he wanted, or how he wanted."

Rufus nodded slowly. "All those things, I've heard. They're not so far off the truth." He tapped his fingers. "I've heard about bad things happening to the people who crossed Johnny. Peter used to tell me stories, you know the kind of thing kids overhear when no one meant them to?"

Ferry got an expression on her face, full of that kind of story, and he immediately curled an arm around her. "Sorry?" he asked.

"I - there was a thing I overheard my parents saying, once. About me and marrying me off. It wasn't very nice. Even if I understood why."

"Oh." And then he had to circle back. "So. Peter told me about how his Da." He stopped and tried again. "How people who didn't do what Johnny said, bad things happened. Nothing - huge, obvious? But their sheep died and their roof blew off, the hens stopped laying. All those things."

Ferry shook her head. "But that's... I mean. That's." She waved her hand. "That's the kind of magic people get blamed for, but it doesn't fit in - how magic works, usually?"

"Do you think people just do magic how the books say?" Rufus was careful here.

"Well. No. I suppose not. But still. There's. Patterns and things."

It was then that they heard a noise, someone coming through the woods.

The rustling turned into the sounds of someone whistling, and then someone getting closer. There was a "Oh, my, didn't mean..." and then a "Feronia Wright, are you doing things your aunt would disapprove of?"

Ferry pushed herself more upright, and returned, "Depends which aunt you ask." It was quite brazen, really.

That got a laugh, and Lord Carillon sketched a bow. "A touch, my lady. I was..." He paused. "Have you seen anyone else about, recently?"

Ferry shook her head, but Rufus said, "A few people, earlier, before I set up here. Going - that way." He pointed deeper into the woods.

"And what's that way, do you happen to know?" The question was easy, light, not pressing, but Rufus suddenly grunted.

Immediately, that easy gaze turned a little sharper. "You've just worked a thing out, you clever boy."

"Not a boy. Sir." The last was through somewhat gritted teeth.

"Pardon." The apology was immediate and sincere enough.

Rufus had to pause, to think around his oath. "You don't know the Forest well yet, sir." Careful, paced. "There's been rumours of several things, that way. A white hart. You know they're held to have special properties."

Carillon nodded. "Liminal, entering other spaces."

"But I'm also hearing other things. Birds. Rare ones, being startled."

Carillon settled a little, rocking on his feet as if he was trying to get his bearing. "Rufus, are you able to tell me if someone made you promise things?"

Ferry said, promptly, "Carillon, he promised he wouldn't tell about a specific conversation. He can talk around it, a little."

"Ah, indeed." And then a "So. Can't you direct me at a thing. Do you want to - continue helping with whatever it was?"

Rufus took a breath, thinking the answer through, and not feeling that agonising contraction of the oath closing in. "No, sir, I don't."

"What will happen to you if you... "

"I swore on my magic, sir. But more than that, if I go against them, won't be worth living in the Forest, sir. They - offered me a way out, sir. Money enough to fix things up. Get my life together."

Carillon thought that over. "They wanted your - power for something, I'm guessing? Oh, no ducking that, young man, I felt it, when you helped me on the road. Unpractised, but quite potent." He glanced at Ferry and grinned. "Pardon the phrasing."

Ferry waved her hand. "I gather it was something about stabilising the bog," she said helpfully.

That got Carillon making a very thoughtful noise, and then drawing out a very large piece of beige silk with dark squiggles. He held the map up with a "So if we're here, and that's there... hmmm." And then a "Is there a chance they were curving around south?"

Rufus considered. "Possible, sir. There's a break in the bog, there, um, between those two bits, bit above where your... um, could you bring it over?"

Carillon obliged, setting the map on a bit of spare blanket. Ferry moved to pin down a corner against the wind.

They got the map down, and weighted with rocks, so they could use it, not fight it. Rufus took a deep breath. "Here we are, sir."

Ferry silently handed him a small white pebble and then held out her hand with several other small heavy objects in it. There was a brown stone, a dark grey one, a bright blue enamel button, a tin soldier that must belong to Caelus, a tiny but heavy ceramic dog.

Rufus glanced at the hand, grinned at her for a moment, and she shrugged. "Children," she murmured.

"This white pebble is where the white hart has been seen, more or less. This button is where the birds are. The tin soldier is the village, the ordinary folk." Non-magical. "But they've got a few people patrolling. The dog is where I think they'll be meeting, but I might be wrong." And then he set the two dark pebbles in two large areas of the map, between the hart and the meeting point, and the meeting point and the sea. "And the dark stones are the bogs in the way."

Carillon peered at it, then extracted glasses from his pocket, and peered at the map some more. "And there's no way round?"

Rufus tapped the map. "If you go this way, there's a

village. Go this way, and you hit the main road. Decent chance someone will come along, and these days, maybe a car or a van or something moving too fast to confound, and too much iron to charm, and..." He shrugged. "More danger than that lot would like."

There was a tap on the other side. "And here?"

"Squire Beaufort's place. He's got nasty dogs."

"And here?" Carillon's voice was thoughtful.

"Steep bank, hard to get ponies down, and a treacherous footing for some of it."

Carillon nodded and considered. Finally, he said, carefully. "So, if they're going to move things quickly in the Forest, between here and there." And he tapped the white pebble and the blue one "And the water, they need to go through the bogs, or spend a lot of time going around."

Ferry offered, tentatively. "I didn't do fauna at school, but - aren't birds and deer both delicate to transport?"

Carillon clapped his hands, suddenly. "There you go, you're brilliant, Ferry, let no one tell you otherwise."

Ferry was startled, wide-eyed. She felt Rufus take her hand and squeeze it, could feel herself flushing.

Carillon glanced at her, and then went on, clearly to spare her further embarrassment. "You're quite right that birds are delicate to transport, and a white hart, to catch and move, as well. So taking the more direct route, that's a thing and one where they could have someone manage them with magic, the whole way. Do you know if they've got anyone who's.." He searched for words.

Ferry squeezed Rufus's hand for a moment. He seemed about to say something, but before he could, Carillon went on.

"Anyone who's good at making things - float. Or lighter. Or something like that?"

Rufus sighed and settled a little, clearly thinking. "Sir." He said, after a moment. "When we were talking in the pub. I mean, they were talking, I was listening."

Carillon said, promptly, "Monday, you mean?"

Rufus startled, and Carillon said, "Monday afternoon, when Johnny paid for your drinks."

"What. Wait. How did you? You." And then it dawned on him. "You were - the man I couldn't see, out by the window."

This got a jaunty little half-salute with his hand. "Useful skill in my line of work." Ferry made a confused noise, and he murmured, "Titch of diplomatic work. A little solving of domestic mysteries. Sneaking down to the kitchen for a biscuit."

Ferry was fairly sure the last one was him teasing. Probably.

Rufus coughed and then said. "So you saw them, more or less. Douglas and Adam, the two who were closer to the window, mostly quiet. Douglas has got a knack with light-ening magics, he's a handy man for balancing a load. And Adam's known for steadying things. Traction, good footing."

Carillon clucked his tongue, thinking again. "Might do it. Might indeed do it. But what to do about it?" He turned his head and looked at Rufus, and Ferry suddenly found the pale blue eyes too demanding, too fierce. "Why haven't you reported this?"

"My oath, sir."

That clearly wasn't sufficient, and Rufus made a strained sound. "I did promise, sir. And it was made on my magic, it's not the law that would make me pay for that."

Carillon just waited. And waited.

Finally, carefully, Rufus said. "The oath, sir. But also, I

don't - actually know for sure. Nothing I could take to a magistrate."

"They're impartial."

This made Rufus make a strangled noise, and then push himself upright for a moment, and have to go away and kick a tree. Ferry leaned to watch him, startled and suddenly rather frightened. It was a minute or so before she said, cautiously, "That'd be a no?"

Carillon settled back, leaning on one hand, and said, carefully. "Magistrates are people, and all people are flawed, it's a question of whether the flaws affect their work. Magistrates are - they're bound by particular oaths, made on their magic, enforced by the Silence. They don't talk about it much, most of them. They don't like to."

"So they are impartial?" Ferry was having trouble following this.

"When they are acting as the magistrate, standing in for Justice and Truth. Well, they're not entirely impartial, but a lot more than when they're having a drink at a party, yes."

Ferry turned a little to watch Rufus, who had kicked the tree again harder, hopped on one foot several times, and then came back, walking a bit unevenly. "Impartial is not the word I would use, sir." And again, there was that rather gritted teeth sound.

"They are impartial within the scope of their oaths. The trick is getting the information to them when they are within that scope. Or finding one who is so inclined in the first place."

Rufus made a gesture, that started out as the rude flick of the fingers of the Forest folk against outsiders. His thumb and ring finger went shooting out before he stopped and put his hand down. "Don't know one I'd trust."

Carillon considered, and said "Daughterty, no, I quite

agree. Sutton - drunken sot, pardon my language, Ferry. Edwards, no, he's married into one of the families I'd rather suspect of bringing things in. Cope - mmm. Possibly, but not this year. No, Rufus, you're right, I quite apologise. No one I'd suggest taking this to. At least not this week."

Ferry murmured "This week?"

"Danforth's due back in two or three weeks, and he's quite reliable."

"Don't know him, sir," was all Rufus said.

"I was posted with him, in the war, for - mmm. Four months and a half, nasty, but he held up well. Good man, listened, which not enough officers do. And he's sharp, which is more than one can say for Daugherty or Sutton."

Rufus paused, and then ventured a careful, "Do you suggest something else, then, sir?"

Carillon tapped his fingers. "I need to figure out which Ministry office smuggling falls under, but there are special magistrates, not associated with a particular area. What I need to do is get on to one of those and get him to hear you out."

Ferry made a noise at the 'him', and Carillon murmured, "In this case, I believe they're all male. Might be wrong. Anyway, someone without local ties, in this case." And then a more serious. "Rufus, if I find someone, will you talk to them?"

Rufus took a deep breath, and there was that moment, feeling what the Silence would do, and then he nodded. "Yes. As much as I can."

Carillon nodded, and then pushed himself to stand, much more lightly than one would expect. Ferry blinked up, startled. "You two enjoy the rest of your afternoon. Rufus, if you find out more you can tell me, you know where I am. I'll leave word at Ytene if you need to get something to me and I'm not there. Often not, really." He sketched a bow to Ferry, with a "My lady, do enjoy the afternoon, you remain both brilliant and delightful, don't ever let anyone change that."

They watched him sweep off with a little puzzlement, the wind rustling his coat as they went.

TWENTY-THREE

NEAR BOAR COURT

They lingered in the meadow a bit too long until it was getting toward twilight. Finally, they had to admit it was getting dark and packed up the blanket and various materials. Ferry slipped the tokens back in her pocket while Rufus adjusted the straps on Star's harness.

"Can I ask where your bits and bobs came from?"

"The dog is Cardea's. She can have it back when she stops poking her brother with it. The tin soldier is his. I - hadn't the heart to tell him war's not like that. The button's from my winter coat. Hand-me-down from a cousin, one of the others broke in half, I need to find something to match the size, next I'm in town."

"Bigger town, I assume?"

"Nanny wants me to make a trip to Trellech soon."

Rufus paused, then said, "Do you know Trellech?" before he turned the pony along the little deer trek toward the road.

"Oh, yes. One of my aunts - um, the aunt I actually really enjoy, Aunt Annonia, she lives there. I like visiting. It's..." Ferry paused. "I've been to London, but the magic's so weak there, it feels funny. Trellech's more like school. I feel like there're foundations under me, old ones, solid. Like Boar Court. I bet Ytene's even more so. It's older by a good bit."

"Older?" Rufus was confused.

"There're theories about magic and places. One of them is that places with lots of people drain off magic faster, so there's less to use. People still can, but it takes - tapping a ley or having some source that's not about the..." She paused, rummaging for the word. "One of my teachers called it the ambient energy."

Rufus mulled this over. "Like, oh, bees having lots of pollen to choose in a meadow, but not if a field's ploughed over or even paved?"

Ferry lit up. "Like that, exactly. Less to choose from."

"And Trellech's not like that?"

"No. Trellech's... always been smaller than the number of people who drain it off. Even with people doing complicated magics. Professor Ottson said that Trellech was made like a dam is, to make a lake. Made so that it would let magic pool and get deeper."

"Huh." Rufus had to think about this more. "Does that make a difference in who lives there?"

Ferry nodded, as they wove their way through the woods, going slow and careful because it was darker and darker. "Mostly - materia practitioners. People who make complicated magical things. And the Ministry, of course, and the Guard headquarters. The things that need a central office. And a lot of that doesn't drain magic off fast. And fancy people have houses. That doesn't either."

"Does your aunt - make things, then? Or do other things?"

"She makes jewellery. All sorts, everything from

apprentice and house pieces to rings or pendants or neck-laces that have specific workings built in."

"Yours?" He was a little cautious asking. He'd known some people who were right touchy about that kind of thing.

"She didn't do the metal - her hands aren't as steady as they used to be. But she put the stone in. She's got appren-tices, they keep her busy." Ferry paused, then said softly. "I'm not good at the metalwork, that's the part she really needs help with. That's why I'm not there."

"So why do you need to go to Trellech?"

"Oh, Nanny has a thing she wants delivered. Private, she said." Ferry put her hand over her mouth. "Sorry, shouldn't even have said that."

Rufus slipped an arm around her waist. "Oh, I've no worries about you being able to keep private what you need."

This was, perhaps, a bad sentence for others to overhear.

It happened in a flurry, as they climbed from the meadow onto the road itself, a sudden burst of people out of the brush at the sides of the road. Rufus felt Ferry pulled away from his side. Though he tried to grab for her, he couldn't reach her, and then there was a blow on the side of his head, and his knees went out. He saw someone grab for Star, and the flash of her white fetlocks in the gloom as she squealed and kicked out before taking off into the night.

He got a knee in the face, then, buffeting him, and a "Knew you couldn't be trusted," before he got a foot in the ribs. "Saw that bloody lord come out from where you were. What'd you tell him, then?"

Rufus tried to look up, get his bearings, and he got

slapped across the face, and the dust was thick enough to make him cough. "Let Ferry go."

It came out entirely plaintive, not at all commanding or sure of himself. And all it brought him was laughter. "Oh, you bastard, we're not letting her go to run off and tell His Lordship all about what happened. And you, oh, we're going to have fun figuring out what to do about you."

Another elbow got his rib, and he was roughly yanked to his feet. He could see Ferry over to one side, someone had a cloth with something over her mouth, and she was going limp, another man catching her. It didn't look like they were hurting her, exactly. At least not going out of their way to hurt her.

Hands pushed his shoulders forward, yanked his hands back, and then he could feel scratchy rope around his wrists. Someone said a word and the ropes tightened, so he could barely wriggle them. The hand jabbed him in the shoulder blades, and another man said another word. When Rufus tried to ask what they were going to do, he found no sound came out. None.

They pushed him along to a cart before they tied a rag over his eyes. He could feel Ferry dumped in beside him, his fingertips just brushing her coat, he remembered what the texture was like, finer and smoother than anything these men wore. Anything Rufus wore.

Two men climbed in the back, a few rough words.

Then the cart was off, and he could do nothing about it. It rolled along, bumping and jostling him and the men guarding him made a few grunted comments as they went, before something or someone hit his head.

TWENTY-FOUR

A LARGE DARK SPACE

He came to in the dark, a single lantern burning. He wasn't sure how long it had been. He was in some kind of storehouse. Larger than a cottage. High ceiling, dark, the smell of damp and mice.

There was a noise, from behind him, someone moving, and he startled, twisting around fast enough to make his head spin more, make him grab for anything to steady himself, to be ready to fight. His heart was pounding, he could barely hear, it was like being back in the trenches again, surrounded and battered from all sides, with death coming.

"Is anyone there?" It took him too long to realise it was a woman's voice. Not someone shouting at him. Not artillery.

"Who's there?" This time it was more nervous, higher, uneven. Trying to be brave, and failing.

Rufus took a deep breath, and then another one, demanding that his body slow down and let him think, let him speak. It worked as badly as it always did when he was like this, and the silence stretched out, and out.

"I can hear you. I know someone's there."

He made a strangled noise, and he heard her cry out, something sharp and high, before there was an uneven. "Who's there, please?"

Another breath, and another. He couldn't hear anyone else around them. No shift of weight or boot leather creaking. Just someone else. Breathing. He shook his head, trying to clear it, trying to get his heart to settle, trying to remember how to be human, not a rabbit trapped by a hawk.

"Please. Why aren't you saying anything?"

The sound was plaintive now, still unsure, but he kept telling himself, shouting it in his head, that this wasn't a threat. Well, probably not.

Things that sounded innocent weren't always. He'd learned that too well. After the stories started circulating after Mons, someone had used that, warped what should be beautiful and safe and pure, into something horrible. A voice on the battlefield, luring people out, with memories of a better time. Lured them out into bullets and death and foulness. A will-o-wisp twisted further by war.

"Please? Are you all right?"

He took another breath, and another, and then ventured looking around, making the shape with his hands that his trenchmate told him would keep evil magic away. He thought this was right, thumb pressed up between his fingers, and he shook it in the direction of the voice.

"Please?" And then there was something else, there, the voice taking a breath, and offering a "You're scaring me."

It was that, finally, that made him shake himself, a dog shaking off the bog muck, try to get a grip on his fear.

"Hello?" he offered. "Can't see much. Only a lantern, back here."

"Rufus. Oh, Nimue's light, is that you?"

He shivered. Was it safe? The shapes in the dark, they'd call your name, too, he remembered that entirely too well.

"Rufus? Tell me that's you, please?"

He paused, then said, carefully, "Not safe to trust - things you hear in the dark." There. That wouldn't give anything away. Not too much.

He heard a sound from her, something he couldn't begin to describe, and then a rustle, of someone trying to move on furniture. "Rufus, they tied me up, I can't move. I'm on a sort of bed. I think." She sounded very dubious about its competency as furniture. Hearing it creak, he had to agree.

"Tell me something only you'd know?"

There was a startled noise, then a "You think I'm not me. Okay. Um. I'm not sure why you do. But I am me. Ferry. Feronia." And then in a rush a "Beltane afternoon, you grabbed my hand, and we ran off to watch the mirabiles, and they were the most beautiful thing I'd seen in such a long time, so much joy. Not - beautiful like artwork you're supposed to like, but breathtaking. Free."

"Stay put. Moment." He took a breath. It was her. It had to be her. A shade wouldn't know that, would they? It had been broad daylight. "Are you all right? Did they - did they hurt you?"

"Nothing like that, you." There was something harsh in her voice for a moment, he couldn't make sense of it, and then, oh. "No wounds, I meant?"

"Oh, no. Some sort of - something, potion, over my mouth? Smelled foul. Made me go all dizzy. I have a rotten headache, but it's getting better. You were - I think you were out a long time."

He took a breath and another, and then he could investigate what they'd done to him. "Bump on my head." He could feel it throbbing, dully, under a raft of other pains and bruises. "Kicked me, I think." He paused, evaluating. "Tied to a chair. But maybe - can you get free at all?"

There was quiet from the corner where she was, then a decided bit of wriggling, that made the thing she was on creak alarmingly. "Don't, if it'll shake that thing apart," he said quickly.

"Maybe. One of my hands... No, give me a minute. I'm going to need to... is it a problem if I use magic?" she asked suddenly.

"No?" he said, a little uncertain. "What - what kind?"

"There's a thing to - loosen fibres. People use it to untangle yarn, but it ought to work enough, here, make the rope flex more. I think." And then her voice was dryly amused. "This is not actually the sort of thing they taught us in school."

He had to laugh at that. "Give it a try. I haven't heard anyone else. So maybe they've left us alone?"

"I wouldn't count on that." She was rather clear in her opinion. But then she settled in, and there was a little humming, an odd repetitive catch to the melody, over and over, repeating three lines of words he couldn't quite hear. It went on and on, lulling him into drifting, his eyes closing.

The next thing he knew, her voice was sounding rough, but there was an insistent repetition, and another, and one more, and then he heard it, the sound of something giving way, and an ominous rumble of the bed frame, then boots hitting the ground and the sound of wooden bars clattering onto a stone floor. The first sound was enough to get him looking toward her, though it was almost totally black, he could only see flickers of movement. "Ferry? Are you all r..."

"Here, love. Right here." There she was, kneeling at his feet, reaching to undo the ties at his wrist, tutting over them, working the rope out of tight knots, insistent and demanding that the hemp do what she wanted.

"Useful magic." He felt awkward. She was rescuing him, this was not how the stories went.

"Turns out, yes." She was focusing hard, the comment was a little abrupt, then a "Give me a minute. Or. Wait, light would help." She stood, leaving him suddenly alone in the dark, and he wanted to cry out, only he wouldn't let himself.

She was back in a moment, with the lantern. Not a lot of candle, mind. "Enough to see this by, I hope. Here, what did they do." He looked down at his hands. "That's a boating knot." He was a bit startled by that.

"Whatever it is, it's very annoying. Just when I think..." She paused, and he could see her, now, in the flickering light, her tongue sticking out slightly, as she chewed on the problem. "Oh, there we are." And then it was a matter of untangling the end and unweaving it from several layers of rope around his wrists. "Free."

He looked up at her. "Like mirables." He was rewarded with a broad flash of a smile before she bent to untie his feet, which was clearly a much easier problem.

Once that was handled, he stretched, carefully. "Nothing broken. Bruised, but not .." He stood up carefully. "Where are we, do you think?"

That got an arch "You know the Forest, I don't," from her. And then she peered around. "Some sort of - barn? Storehouse? Do you think we're locked in?"

He stood up and moved carefully. "Long. Narrow. Tithe barn, I think." He pauses. "So. Wait. We should think about this."

"Can you - figure out if there's anyone out there?"

He paused, and then said, cautiously, "Never did it for real." His voice got quieter and quieter.

She was quiet, then said, "What do you mean by that?"

"Master Burleigh told me I could learn it. And we did a little, but ... I've never been sure it worked right. That it wasn't dumb luck. Or just knowing the forest."

There was a pause, then Ferry said, thoughtfully. "Bear with me, working through a theory. You can - make a bog steady, right? Bogs have lots of water in them. So do people. Can you feel if there's something like that out there?"

He considered, then said "That's not how he had me do it?" He could see where she was going wiht the idea, though.

"But I'm good with water. Not just the bogs, finding streams and things. Let me - try?" He settled back in the chair, did his best to ignore the dull headache, and closed his eyes. "Something - bigger. Not a person. That way. Something - maybe a person, there? Maybe a dog, with him." He pointed the opposite way.

"Do you know about dogs?"

"A bit. If they left one, it's probably a guard dog. Or there's traps. Something to stop us getting out."

She made an uncertain noise and then said "Let's think this through. Before trying anything."

"There you go, being sensible. Glad one of us is."

"Do you have an idea where we are, then?"

He considered. "Not Beaulieu. That's bigger. Cleaner. Used more. Not ... can you feel the Silence? The places it protects?"

She blinked up at him, he could just see it in the lantern. Then she nodded. "Maybe," she said. "It makes a sort of... not-sound. A hum, only you can't actually hear it?"

He was startled "You mean all the time?"

She shrugged. "I got used to it when I was at school. I think I only noticed it when I was there. Where I grew up, people know where the house is. They just don't come down the drive." She closed her eyes, leaning her hand on the table, doing something that wasn't quite concentrating.

"I hear it. Feel it. Fairly clear. And like..." A pause. "This is a little hard to tell. But like we're in the middle of a Silence-cloaked area, not on an edge? Like it's blanketing all over."

He nodded, regretted moving his head, then said: "There's - only a couple of barns we might be in then."

She waited, then when he didn't continue, said "Tell me about them? The possibilities?"

"Possibly down near Allum. Possibly west of Ytene. Possibly a bit north of where we were, up by Landford. I wish I hadn't that knock on my head, so I knew how far we went."

Ferry made a face. "So, three places across the north half of the Forest, then. Nothing to narrow it down?"

He had to laugh. "You've been learning, love."

She stuck her tongue out, and then laughed as well. "So, what does that mean? How do we." She paused. "What do we do when we get out? We need a plan, you."

"We get out. We go find someone to report things to. One of the magistrates. This is more than just - rumour."

Ferry made a considering noise. "You know, probably the magic left traces. Enough, if we find someone fastish."

"And there's stopping them, with the smuggling, that's a thing we need to do before next nightfall."

"So. Nothing complicated then. We have to escape a locked building that's stood for several centuries already so is probably quite solid. Then we have to get past a dog and a guard, well, probably a dog and a guard. And then we have to find our way in the dark with no light across some amount of open ground to an unknown location."

Rufus interrupted. "Should be able to find somewhere safe in True Eyeworth. Or at Boar Court. Or Ytene. Which-ever we're nearest."

"Which, we don't know, so that's still not simple."

"Know the Forest well enough. We get clear, I can get my bearings, I can figure it out." He did his best to sound sure, but he wasn't nearly as certain as he sounded.

Ferry let out a puff of breath, and he watched her, uncertain. "I suppose that will have to do." And then a "How are we getting out of here?"

Rufus drummed his fingers on the chair, looking around. Solid door here. Solid door there. Probably with dog and guard. Window, wrong side. And then he paused, and looked up, and said, "How are you at climbing, then?"

TWENTY-FIVE

TITHE BARN

Ferry looked at him. "Climbing?" she asked, and then she looked up. Rafters, and then - oh. What looked like beams and thatch over. "You're thinking we can get out through the thatch? But what about the dog? And the guard?"

Rufus shrugged. "One thing at a time. Guessing the door's barred, and the windows will make a noise."

Ferry considered the problem. "Skirts are not really made for climbing," she points out "And there's not much light."

"Thought they taught you things, in school?" It came out harsher than he meant, she hoped, because that had quite the edge to it, and she winced.

"Not one one I'm much good at."

Rufus stood up, then sat down, and said "That." His voice was tight. "That is a bloody useful skill. How are you not good at it, woman?"

Ferry shifted, wanting to pull away, to run, but there was nowhere to run to, except the end of the dark barn. That would be ridiculous and do no one any good.

"I..." She stopped. Everything she might say here sounded awful. That she didn't need to be good at it. They had people to manage the lights at home, and at Boar Court.

He was just watching her. He crossed his arms over his chest, and he was near glaring at her. "Well?"

"It's a - specialised skill." Careful, slow, thinking it out. "We learn it, but it's - not..." And then a "Of course you'd think it was amazing. It's really practical some places. But not where I've been."

"I," Rufus said, his voice tight "Have just figured out how to be fairly sure there's someone with a large dog out there. And you figured out how to use a spell designed for untangling yarn to get us loose. So. You'll not be telling me you can't figure out a bit of light."

She stood, suddenly, taking the three or four steps she could into the dim gloom, an aisle between stored boxes, and then she looked around. "Rufus." It was quick. "Why do you think they put us here?"

Rufus considers. "Safe, out of the way?"

"Maybe it's where they're hiding the other things they're smuggling? Some of them? Don't they still need you for the bogs, one way or the other?"

A horrible thought occurred to both of them at the same time. "Keep you hostage, for my helping?"

She nodded. "Otherwise, why keep us both?"

Rufus looked up sharply, and said, "I thought I was the one who'd gone to War and seen men thrown away?"

Ferry shivered. "They..." And then she stopped. That didn't matter. That she wasn't allowed to be there. It wasn't the same. Instead, she said, "More than one way to throw people away, Rufus. Most of them are much less - obvious."

There was a long silence. It got longer and longer.

Finally, out of the dark, behind her, she heard "Fair enough. And it doesn't get us out of this barn."

She let out a long sigh of relief. "No, it doesn't. So. I can try a light. I don't promise it will work, but I'll do my best. Before I do, could they see, through the windows?"

Rufus muttered "Probably."

"Do we need the light? Can we take the lantern?"

He shook his head. "Risk of fire, that near the thatch. That's no good."

"Let, no, that won't work." She was thinking out loud, now. "Can we get me up on that beam? Or whatever one we want to work from? I can try a light up there where it won't carry so much."

He nodded, then said "Help me look around. See if there's anything might help with the climbing." She took the candle, and followed him, holding it so he could peer over piles of wood and boxes.

"Bloody hell," he said, after a moment looking at something.

"What is it, then?" She couldn't tell, it was a pile of wooden cases, latched. Rufus reached to touch one, ran his fingers along the label. "If I'm right, this is - there are orchids, rare ones, grow in the wood. Used for potions."

He moved down, then a "And..." These cases were larger, about the size of something that might hold a cat or puppy. He knelt down, one knee on the ground of the barn, in the dirt. She watched him run his fingers along the case, unlatch it, and then open the case. Inside, packed in something soft she couldn't make out, there was a brilliantly coloured bird, feathers in an irridescent blue.

"A twilight nightjar, that is. Rare as anything. Hide in trees in the day, blend into t'night sky. Like owls or hawks, only they eat berries, not mice." He paused, and

Ferry watched him, saw there was something complicated there.

"They sing. All nightjars do, a sort of - murmuring. Vibrating. Little like a cat's purr, more than birdsong, but..." He gestured. "The twilight ones, they're magic. Look at the feathers, how they shimmer? Their eggs, they get used for things or used to. That was in the book, you remember?"

He was so painfully earnest about it, Ferry wasn't sure what to do.

"What - what do we do about them?"

He made a strangled noise. "They're... I suppose there are magics - no, I know there are, some people use them for keeping food. I remember that." She could hear the edge of panic in his voice, trying to work it out. "Oh, they - this isn't right, Forest, this isn't right." His pitch was rising.

She came around, knelt beside him, took his hand. "We can't - free them. I don't know the right thing, and birds are fragile, aren't they? So the best thing we can do is what we were doing, get free, find help, someone who can - stop this."

Rufus settled back on his knees, took a shaky breath, then another. "You're right. I know you're right. I just wish you weren't."

Ferry squeezed his hand, waited another three breaths, and then said "Come on. More to look at. Maybe we'll get lucky and there'll be a ladder."

She said it not thinking they'd be that stupid, but they made their way down one side of the barn, half the other, and then she blinked. "There, Rufus, do you see? Do you think maybe..."

It was old, they could see that, but it was hooked along the wall, long enough to reach the rafters if they positioned it right. Rufus gestured for her to take the part that was easier to get to. He bent to move boxes, doing it quickly and carefully, until he could get the other end free. "Here, over here," he said. "Dog's that way."

Together, they propped it up, and he said, "You first." She blinked at him, in the flickering light, and he said "You're lighter. If something happens, I can catch you. Hold it steady." He paused, then said "Here, bring this rope up with you. In case the ladder goes."

She nodded, murmuring a "You think ahead. Thank you." And then she tucked her dress up, using her scarf to hold it, blessing the fact she favoured skirts with plenty of fabric. She looped the coil of rope over her shoulders, shivering at the weight of it, took a breath, and climbed.

The ladder was rickety, there was no doubt about that, but it held well enough under her if she went slow and careful. Rung by rung, over and over, concentrating on going up, and up, until she could reach the broad beam across the top, then edge herself over toward the side of the barn. Rufus, below, gestured for her to move to the other side. She did, cautious and slow, before he began to climb.

Watching him was terrifying, she could see the ladder shift and bow as he climbed, see him taking each rung slower than she had, waiting for it before shifting his weight. He was finally up when there was a crack, and it started to go, a rung at least. He heaved himself onto the beam, stomach flat on the wood, hanging over it.

Everything was utter quiet for a moment, and then nothing fell, nothing shattered. He was right there. And he began to pull himself up, to turn to sit, using the beam against the roof to help him.

"Merlin," she said, letting out a breath. "That was a near thing." And then a "Now we're here. What do we do?"

"Make a light, then, can you? We're far up, they won't see from the window even if they look."

Ferry nodded and took a deep breath. She thought back to that moment. The classroom in the keep, the benches and desks. The smell of the wood polish. She inhaled and exhaled. All the lessons she'd been taught. About the magic swirling inside you, about giving it directions, being clear. The words of clarity, the ones that had been used so long they had their own power to shape the magic a particular way.

She cupped her hands in front of her, and then brought them up to her mouth, and murmured "Lux" as she breathed into her hands. "Fiat lux."

Nothing happened for a moment. She felt a sudden sinking feeling, despair, and then the something in her that wanted, that needed, much more urgent. She closed her eyes and said it one more time, barely a whisper. "Fiat lux."

Rufus gasping made her open them again. In her hands was a glowing light, not so bright as to blind them, but clear and steady. "Oh. Ohhhhh." She couldn't stop staring at it.

Rufus was watching her now, not the light, when she looked away and blinked. "Thought you'd done before?"

She shook her head slightly, shivering for a moment. "Did a - like a little tiny candle flame, flickering. Held it for a little. Nothing like that. Nothing like - it's so clear and steady. I didn't know I could do that." And then she murmured "It - I should be able to put it where we want it. It doesn't burn things, I can hold it in my hand. Not fire."

Rufus shook his head slightly, about to say something, and then he didn't. "Try that, then." Gentle and reassuring.

She reached out, setting the light by the beam so they could see. "Ah, there we go," Rufus said, approving. "That gives us a good look. Right. We'll be wanting that rope, and we'll be wanting this. Careful, won't do me good if we drop it." And he reached into a pocket low on his trousers and pulled out a small folding knife.

"You've a knife? But why - didn't you, before?"

"Couldn't reach it. Peter..." His voice caught for a moment. "Peter taught me, keep two. One kept somewhere they'll look for it, one somewhere where they won't. Guessing that's not something he learned from his Da."

Ferry made a stifled noise. "Oh." She said. "So we have a knife. And we have a light. And a rope. What's the plan, then? You have a plan?" She very much wanted someone to have a plan, and it wasn't her.

"Using this light," Rufus grinned. "I look for a patch of thatch we can cut through. Cut a hole big enough for us. Tie the rope to the beam. Lower ourselves down, careful. Get out into the woods, find somewhere safely away for the next step."

"Put like that, seems almost child's play."

"Not afraid of heights, I hope?" He was doing his best to play it lightly and she appreciated that.

"No, no. But I'll be glad for getting through this fast."

He nodded. "Let me see what we can be doing, then." He shifted to straddle the beam, then to loop the rope and attach it to give him extra to brace himself, so that overbalancing wouldn't send him falling down. Careful and attentive, like he'd been up in high spaces doing terrifying things before.

All she could do was sit and watch and not get in the way.

It took him maybe a quarter of an hour, and then there was a quiet "Here we go. Let me - let me focus. See if they've moved." He went quiet and still again, rubbing his forehead for a moment, then there was a "No, back there. Right. Better done sooner."

TWENTY-SIX

TITHE BARN

Rufus spent a few more minutes getting things sorted out to his satisfaction. Ferry watched him, appreciating the care and attention. Despite the urgency, despite the need, he didn't rush; he checked things, three times each. The slit in the thatch went high and low enough for someone his size to step through. The rope around the beam inside, to be fed outside and let them work their way down.

"Can you climb down a rope?"

She frowned. "It's another thing I've not done often," she admitted. "And not in skirts."

"I could lower you down. Or I could go down first, and help you. Do you..." His voice trailed off.

Ferry took a deep breath. "I think I can manage. I hope. And... you're better off running if you hear the dog. They're... I think they're less likely to hurt me? Maybe?"

Rufus looked at her, quiet for a long moment. "Maybe," he agreed, finally. Then, a little fussy "I wish we had more rope, a shorter piece, to make a harness with." Something then gave him an idea, and he worked to find the end of the long rope, eyeing how much extra there was. He began making looping knots in it, every five feet or so, spreading out his arms to measure.

"They'll - help us climb down. Slide your feet to the next knot, bring your hands as low as you can as you lower your feet, climb down a bit, to the next knot. Can't do more, the rope's not long enough, but will let you pause, get your breath."

She nodded. "You - you think of everything."

Rufus grinned at her, she could see so clearly in the light. "So we hope," he said. "Here, let me get the rope through, check one more time we can't see anyone this side of the building."

She nodded. "Where do we go when we're down?"

"Depends where we are. Should be able to tell - even in the dark - by the space around the barn."

"Right. I - we can do this. Tell me we can do this." She was suddenly terrified.

Rufus reached out for her hand, reassuring. "We can do this. Together. Couldn't have got free without you. I'll do my part now. Right?"

She smiled weakly but nodded. "Right."

Then he was pressing himself through the thatch, pausing where he could look out, and there was a murmured "Clear." She could feel more than hear him work his way down, the way the thatch shifted back, and the rope had a sudden tension in it. Ferry worked her way standing, shifting around her skirts, terrified she'd catch a foot or knee in fabric and fall. She kept holding onto the great support beam, until she could brace herself and peer out the thatch.

Ferry couldn't see much, just the thatch itself, so she did her best to let that distract her. She fell into a sort of trance, seeing how it connected and wove. The underlayer, that the rest was woven through, how it overlapped to make the roof watertight. She let her hand trace along the lines, feeling it as much as seeing it.

It was at least three or four minutes before the rope went slack, and then had a gentle tug on it. She waved a hand into the dark, before turning to ease herself out, holding onto the rope. Ferry got her hands on one knot, then felt with her feet for the next, down and down and down.

She glanced below her at one point, and froze, it was such a long way. It was dark, and the wind was picking up, and she didn't know if she could keep going. Ferry had to breathe, several times, then remind herself that she couldn't go back from here.

Hand by hand, she went, bumping against the side of the barn. No noise, but she was sure it would leave a bruise and she had to bite her lip to keep from crying out. Her skirts kept trying to tangle in the rope, so she had to stop and wait, hanging there with her arms aching.

She just kept going, like putting one foot in front of the other but horribly disorientated. Suddenly her feet hit something and it was the ground, and her knees were collapsing under her.

Rufus was right there. She couldn't see him - there was no moon she could see, but she could feel him, his arm around her, a soft whispered, "This way. Go careful, don't break branches." He led her off, giving her enough space so she could pick her way along, but staying close enough she knew right where he was.

It seemed to be a road, or at least a track, that led from the barn to a larger road. It wasn't until they'd turned onto that, and a good distance past the turnoff, that he paused, and turned around. "We're up near Landford. But I had a thought."

She froze. "A problem?" It didn't quite come out in a squeak, but it was a near thing.

"Can't get to Ytene without going through the village, or awfully close. And if we do, there'll be people who might spot us, know we're free."

She grimaced and then realised he couldn't see it. "So. So..." She couldn't figure out what to ask.

"Can't get to my cottage, either. Same problem."

"One of the magistrates?"

"Cope would give us shelter, pass us on to the right people, I think, but - he's also near the village, a bit south. Too close for comfort. Too hard to sort out in the night - in the daylight, we might manage better. Circle around to the cottage, take horses from there."

"Boar Court?" she offered, after a moment's thought.

"They'll not like you bringing a scruffy peasant in, right? And people might come looking for us."

"Don't want to - put them at risk. And they lock up pretty early at night." Ferry chewed on her lip. "They won't like me being out all night, either. They must be worried."

"Once we find someone we can trust, we can sort that bit out." He sounded more sure than Ferry felt, by miles.

She considered, then said, "The summer house, at the folly."

"Folly?"

"Silly word for a - sort of fancy playhouse, almost? Lots of windows. Might be a bit chilly yet, but it's private, we could see people coming, ages away."

He grunted, considering, then there was a "Where is it from the house?"

Ferry paused, thinking through it. "You know how the drive goes up, north? And then there's a stream, runs down toward the house from the northeast? It's up by where the stream loops."

"This side of the house, then. That's good. That's real good. Do you mind getting your feet wet?"

She made a startled noise. "Why?" It came out plaintive.

"Good way to get hounds off our scent. If they try. Come on, I know where we're going now, near enough."

TWENTY-SEVEN

NEAR BOAR COURT

Rufus wondered if he had misjudged.

It had been a long walk, several miles, circling around Landford proper, keeping just off the road. No light to speak of, chill air, and the constant worry about sounds behind them.

Ferry hadn't complained, but he could feel her dragging even before they got to the stream. He had to urge her to take her shoes and stockings off and tuck up her skirts again, to ease her way along in the cold water. The stones were smooth under their feet, but slippery.

"Can you make a little light? Will anyone see?"

Ferry looked up, wide-eyed. "Safe?" she asked, breathless.

"For long enough to get to the folly, maybe. So we can see the ground."

Ferry closed her eyes, and did something odd with her breath, then nodded, looking at him, not that they could see much of each other. "I can. For a couple of minutes."

Rufus nodded. "Enough to get us there."

Her eyes closed again, and she cupped her hands, sheltering them in front of her body. Then there was a small light, rather smaller than before, but just as clear and steady. She set it in the curve of her bodice like she was wearing a glowing pendant.

He nodded at her, and together, they worked their way down through the water. Both slipped more than once, getting soaked well above the knees. He kept wanting to offer her his arm, but he was none too steady himself, and if one of them fell, they'd both go down.

They came around a curve of the stream, and he paused, then whispered "Where?"

Ferry closed her eyes, and he thought for a minute she would faint or scream or do something else he couldn't begin to cope with.

"There." She pointed, off a little to the northwest. "That way."

He nodded. "Not so far now, then. Here, take my hand. Here's a rock. Put your shoes and socks on." He let her have the rock, awkwardly standing on one foot then the other as he did the same.

She got her shoes on, then picked up the light from her bodice, and gestured with it for a moment.

They made it across a clear patch of ground, perhaps twenty or thirty feet of grass and flower beds, to the door of the folly. He caught glimpses, stone arches, high windows with glass, what looked like a greenhouse on one side, what looked like a loft above.

It made no sense to him, as a house, as a place people might use. Who made a house three or four times the size of his family's cottage, half a dozen separate rooms at least, to play in? To use a few days a year for parties.

Ferry knew where things were. She led the way in, to an interior hall, murmured. "Close the door." Then she handed him the light, and went carefully through the rooms, closing curtains, testing the edges, then murmured "Come up the stairs with me?"

He was baffled again, but when he got to the top of the stairs, he saw it opened up into a room with a broad daybed in one corner. Ferry was closing the curtains over the arched windows, then running her hand along each one, and they seemed to hold in place.

"No one should see the light now." She turned to face him, and there was something jubilant about her. Her hair was coming out of its tidy bun in wisps and curls, her cheeks glowing pink from the exertion. "Sealed them to the wall."

He inhaled, something unsettling him, and then word-lessly held out his hands with the light. She took it, cupping her hand under it, and moved to a lantern, using the light to find a box of matches. She lit the lantern, set the glass black in place, and set the whole thing on a table by the stairs. It flickered, bathing the room in a warm glow, and she dismissed the light in her hands with a quiet, "Thank you."

"We'll be cosy here. They use it for parties, in the summers when the family's here. Fairly, um, decadent parties. The children and I come and play, sometimes, but no one does more than air it out otherwise."

Rufus rubbed his hands over his face. "There - um. Facilities?" he asked, blushing. She blushed as well and said "Back downstairs. Here, here's another lantern. You can get there without showing a light, the windows have shutters at the back. Just avoid the front rooms, those face the house." And then a "Probably some food in the kitchen, in keep-fresh boxes. Should be, anyway."

He nodded. "Do you - need the facilities?" That was the proper word, maybe, for what he meant.

Ferry gestured at him. "You first. I'll come down, though, see about the food."

It took them a good twenty minutes, but they eventually climbed the stairs again, cleaner, more comfortable. They'd liberated a loaf of bread along with cheese and a summer sausage from the food boxes. A reasonable meal, especially when combined with a bottle of elderflower cordial left in a cupboard.

Ferry poured out two glasses of it and lifted hers. "To a grand escape."

He had to laugh. "A grand escape I couldn't have done without you."

Ferry had settled on the bed, tucking her feet up under a blanket. "Still a bit chilly. That stream. Merlin."

"You all right, though?"

She nodded. "A few bruises on my feet, maybe. Nothing bad."

Rufus let out a breath he wasn't aware he'd been holding. "Good. Warm enough?"

Ferry almost said something, and then said, "I was thinking it would be a good time to curl up with you." Her tone was thoughtful, considering.

He blinked. "Curl up?"

Ferry gestured. "We can't go anywhere until dawn at best. It's - what, the clock said, half past midnight. I'm sure I can't sleep." And then a "There's a potion downstairs if we need it. For being awake in the morning. And my watch has an alarm on it." There was something sharply bright in her voice.

Rufus said, carefully. "And you..." He didn't begin to know how to ask what he needed to know.

Ferry laughed and said "Giddy with - a lot of things. With the magic in me, like it's waking up. With escaping.

Doing it with you. Working with you. Together. It - it makes me..."

She shook her head, and then reached for the pins still in her hair, doing their best to hold it up, and shook her hair free. "We've got a bed and time, and..." Then there was a sudden shyness. "I liked what we did in the meadow. And I - all the time we've been here, I've been thinking about more of that. Now we're free to. And have privacy."

Rufus couldn't help leaning forward, and then there's a "Are you - what do you want, then? Specific?"

Ferry closed her eyes for a long moment, he kept watching her, afraid he'd miss something crucial. Then she looked at him, square on, with a "I want you. I want sex with you. I'm afraid that if I don't, this is... This will turn into some dream and never have happened. And I don't want that. Or at least, if it is a dream, I want - I want to know..." She stopped and blushed red. "I want to know about that kind of magic."

He had to laugh, then. Not at her, and it was clear she understood that almost immediately. At the ridiculous situation that brought them here. To an absurd and contrived ornamental house in the middle of a field in the depths of the Forest.

"Right." He rubbed his face. "Do you? I mean."

"There's a charm for women. To keep us safe. Several kinds." She was so prompt with that he knew she had to have been thinking about it. "I've been using it - well. Since just after May Day. Pross made sure I was doing it right."

Rufus closed his eyes. "So. We - together." He had to stop, and swallow, at the images that brought up in his head. Images of her stretched out in the glow of the lantern, her hair loose on the pillow, her skin under his hands, of her eagerness, her delight. He hoped her delight.

"You know - first times are sometimes really awkward?" That wasn't the word he wanted, he knew.

That got her to laugh. "Awkward was getting carried off and kidnapped and having to escape. Pretty sure this is less awkward. People do it all the time."

He had to bury his face in his hands at that, get a grip on himself, and then there was a "You are an exceedingly practical sort of woman. You know that, yes?"

That got a rather cheerful "I have been told so, yes. So, what do we do?"

Rufus kept a grip on the larger plan. "We. All right, we enjoy ourselves, yes. You set that watch for - just before five. Dawn's right around then. And can you go fetch the potions, so they're right here if we need them?"

Ferry nodded, and went off, back downstairs. She was only gone a minute or two and came up the stairs carrying a large pitcher of water and two small bottles, setting them on the table.

By then, he had a plan. "So. At dawn, we head off, skirting the main roads. I think our best chance is to skirt down, south of Fritham," The nearest non-magical town. "Back roads, to near my fam's cottage. See if we can get one or two of the ponies and go to Ytene from there. Can't cut straight across, too much chance people will spot us."

She settled on the bed, her skirt poofing up. "You don't think they'll be near your cottage? Watching for us?"

He winced. "Can't be everywhere. And some of them'll have jobs, and they'll be finishing up getting the cargo ready. We can go careful? The ponies - Star likes a meadow southeast of there. She got free. Maybe she went there. You need a saddle, don't you? To ride?"

Ferry considered. "I could try without it, but I'd rather not risk it. Not in skirts."

He snorted, then said, "I suppose you didn't really dress for a trek across the Forest."

She laughed and said. "I was rather aiming at having less clothing between me and you touching me, you know. So no bloomers."

He couldn't help it but had to laugh again, and a "Wanting my hands on you, were it? And we got distracted, didn't we? Since you've convinced me you've thought of all the important parts." Ferry beamed at him, and oh, he wanted more of that. Her approval.

She stretched, then said "Would you be so kind as to help me out of my clothes? And I can help you with yours?"

TWENTY-EIGHT

THE FOLLY AT BOAR COURT

F erry couldn't help watching him. His face was expressive. Much more so than he realised, she suspected. Right now it was a mix of wanting and nerves. Caution.

The caution was a thing she loved in him. She'd known boys at school who'd have gone charging off, heedless. She'd known boys who'd logic their way into a corner and get stuck. The ones who'd be all bravado and show, and not practical at all. The ones who were all about what it'd get them, their own advantages and pleasures. Even among her own house, where they tended to be more steady, well, stallions made a show of power and strength and virility.

Rufus did none of that. He doubted himself, his skills, that was clear. And yet, here, he had no reason to. She'd felt that herself, out in the meadow. By the tree. But there was something so steady about him, determined.

His fingers had begun undoing her bodice, button by button. She inhaled sharply as the back of his hand brushed the curve of her breast, and she found him looking at her.

"You tell me if you don't like something. Need a pause."

"Oh, no, not that." The words tumbled out, that was the last thing she wanted. And then she said "What... would you like? Can you tell me?"

That made him shiver, a "You give me everything." And then a softer, almost shy. "Was thinking of what you'd look like, laying back, hair spread out under you. Could you, maybe?" and a little gesture of his fingers at her hair and the bed.

Ferry smiled so broadly, and said "Oh, yes." She could feel herself warming as he worked his way down the bodice. She reached back to shake out her hair properly then wriggled her shoulders, letting the dress begin to fall off her shoulders.

He grinned back at her, and then inhaled, as his eyes dropped, and fixed on her chest. He brushed the chemise aside, and a "Oh, that's grand, love." Then his hand was cupping her breast, lifting and his thumb stroking, sending a shooting desire through her. She wanted urgently to spread herself out, let him look and touch, and do all sorts of things she didn't have words for yet.

She took a few more moments to begin to work on his vest's few buttons, loosen the laces of his shirt. Nothing fancy for him, plain cloth, worn and smooth. He paused in his touching of her to murmur "Stand, m'lady, please? So I can help you undress? All the way?"

Ferry wasn't sure her feet would hold her, but she took his hand as he stood too. Then his hands were undoing the waistband of her dress, and then it was dropping off her, and she could shrug out of the chemise. Suddenly it hit her she was entirely naked, and with Rufus, and this was utterly and unmistakeably real.

He reached out, with a "Hey, love. Just what you want."

Ferry swallowed hard, and then deliberately dropped

her hand, to reach to touch where she could see the swell of his cock now he was just in trousers. He closed his eyes and groaned, arching his back, pressing into the touch.

"Won't leave you wanting." It wasn't what she'd expected to say, but true, all the same. And then, feeling a sudden impishness. "Won't be left wanting, either."

That made him laugh, and a "Oh, my, Ferry, you're a grand witch, aren't you?" He drew her against him, hugging her tightly, beginning to nuzzle and kiss at her neck and ear. His left hand wandered down her body, cupping the curves, as his other worked on his trousers. It took a few moments, then she could feel him pushing the clothing down, stepping away, while all her attention was on the hard heat pressed between them.

"There, oh, there." He was murmuring over and over, a steady stream of words to reassure her. That was not what she needed, not now, and she tugged him, back toward the bed, feeling it hit the back of her thighs.

He laughed against her skin, and then he was pulling the blankets back and away, before helping her lie down on her back. He settled himself beside her, with a "Let me explore you, love, then."

What he did with his kisses and his hands inflamed her. He was deliberate, gentle, working his way down from ear to breast, his hands caressing hip and then encouraging her to spread her legs. "Let me touch you, love, help you get ready for me."

She couldn't help feeling him rock against her, little unconscious shifts of his hips to rub. It must feel good to him, the way it made his breath catch from time to time. Ferry got her eyes open to watch him, his ginger hair hiding his head, then murmured. "Kiss me?"

Something in that startled him, delighted him, and he

shifted, all in a rush, to settle his legs between hers, to press up on his elbows. All the strength of his shoulders was visible at once, his eyes gleaming before he bent to kiss her. Oh, she could feel him, there, so hard and ready, but waiting for her to catch up to him.

His tongue pressed into her mouth, and there was the initial moment where she forgot how this worked, and then remembered, opened to it, encouraged him, responded. It made his hips rock, and she cried out.

Rufus pulled back, and she couldn't bear it, tugging with a hand in his hair to bring him back, make him keep going. She heard a muffled "Oh, that," before he was kissing her again, making her arch beneath his body, press closer, bring her hips to his.

She lost track of time with the kissing and the touching, and the rocking. Eventually, he shifted, reaching between them, letting his fingers stroke at her, at her entrance, and it made her shiver.

"There, love. Nice and ready for me. Feel you, feel you're damp. Wanting. May I, please?"

It made her gasp, the asking, the anticipation of the moment, then she had to try to get her mouth to make words, nodding, then managing a "Please."

Rufus pressed up on one arm, the other down between them, and then she could feel him, right there, the head hard and round and so very real. He paused for just a moment, then he began to press into her.

It didn't hurt, that wasn't the right word, it was something else, stretching and new and strange. He kept rocking in, moving in tiny relentless movements to push, ease back, push, ease back. She held her breath, not meaning to, until he murmured "Breathe, love, it'll help. There, so good, you feel grand, oh, yes."

It was the breathiness in his voice that helped. How awed he sounded. Amazed. That she was doing this right, enough of it. That they both wanted this. She took a breath and let it out. As she did, he slipped in further, more than he meant, maybe, and she cried out, loud in the quiet room, then heard him groan.

He buried his face in her shoulder, his right hand moving to cup her hip. He shifted, trying to keep it slow and easy, but managing for only a few strokes before his desire broke through, and he went deeper or faster.

The uneven strokes made her whimper, had her clinging to his back with one hand, fingers digging into the muscle. It wasn't until he was all the way inside her, filling her up, that she could rebalance, get both arms around him, hold him close, and murmur a "Oh, oh, please."

It wasn't all the things she wanted to tell him, but it was enough. She heard him inhale, breathe her in, and then a "Oh, Ferry, love, grand, oh, yes." His hips began to move, more steadily. "Like that, yes, oh, so good. Tight, so tight."

It made her shiver, the neediness in his voice like he was drinking her down. She wasn't sure what to do with her hands, or her legs, did she lie here, or hold him, she wasn't sure what it would do.

He rocked in, pulled out, pressed back, a dozen times, before he realised her uncertainty, and murmured. "Everything you do is grand. Touch. Hold. Kiss. Leg round me. If you..." She attempted it, winced at a shift, then something settled, and she let out a higher sound, trailing, and felt his cock jerk inside her.

She loved how it felt, how he was rubbing against something inside her that made her feel like magic, fuller and needier, driving her up and on. She got the other leg up around his hip, and then he could move freely. He made a thrust, testing her reaction, then another.

Something in them broke open at the same time, shaking their caution and patient exploration. She was clinging to him, and he was thrusting into her, faster and faster in sharp movements. His breath was uneven, mingled with occasional endearments, comments. "So tight." And "Fuck, so good."

Ferry didn't know how to urge him on, how to tell him this was good. She could hear herself make sounds, high moans and gasps, but not words. All she could do was cling, and roll her hips, and feel him touch deep inside her. It made her ache in a way she hadn't known would feel so good.

It built and built until he was thrusting faster and faster, needy and demanding, his lips sucking at her shoulder, her skin. Suddenly, he was pushing into her. She could feel his cock jerk and pulse, and then a great hot wetness inside her as his hips jerked.

He rocked several times inside her, before he let out a sound, and tried to get his hand between them. "Let me, love, let me, oh..." that was almost incoherent. She was arching, wanting something she didn't know how to get, and then his fingers were there. Somehow, they found the place she needed pressure, a few rubs. Then she was bucking, tightening around him, feeling like she needed the weight of his body to keep her from flying apart.

TWENTY-NINE

THE FOLLY AT BOAR COURT

Rufus felt he was dreaming. Here she was, so trusting. Here he was, and oh, how good that felt. It had been far too long. It wasn't just the sex, the climax. Those were grand.

It was how she'd given herself over to the pleasure that got him. He propped himself on an elbow, just watching her, letting her drift in the aftermath. Once she was drowsing, he reached just enough to get one of the potion bottles, so he wouldn't fall asleep. It was so tempting, just to curl up with her and ignore the world.

Perhaps fifteen minutes later, she opened her eyes and blinked at him. "Watching?" she asked.

"Oh, yes." He couldn't help it coming out in a warm purr. "You're beautiful."

Ferry blushed, and ducked her chin, then watched him a little more. "You honestly think that."

"I'd not lie to you. Not about that." It baffled him someone might.

She waved a hand "Not the sort of figure I'm supposed

to have. Or the hair. Should be lighter or darker, I guess, to be fashionable."

Rufus snorted. "Like you as you are, ta." He shifted to run a hand down her side, tracing the curve over her body. "Do you need anything?"

She made a noise and said. "Handkerchief, and something to tuck it in? Should be one by the pitcher."

He blinked at her. "That's a tad specific?" And then he was looking for it and turning to bring it to her.

"Women's magic." She sounded amused, and he looked back at her, to see she was grinning at him. Ferry said, after a moment. "There's magic in the first time someone has sex. Save the - um, fluids. On a cloth. Use it for magic later."

He considered this, handing the cloth over. "What kind of magic?"

"Nothing that would hurt you. Or bind you." Ferry was quick to say that, he noticed, and he smiled back at her. "Things about - being an adult. Making choices. Some people use them for warding or protection charms, for where they live. Some people use them for making a life they want. Professional things."

Rufus settled on the bed again and said "Huh. Is there a reason?"

"My body's the one thing I can choose to give that's all my doing. I mean, my parents started, but I'm my own person. So there're traditions that build on that. I think for men, too, but I don't know about those. Or if there's other things out there. This is just the one I know. My aunt taught me. The one I like. And Pross."

Ferry used the handkerchief to clean herself up, folding it into a tidy little roll of fabric. She set it by her watch on the table, then settled back on the bed. Rufus shifted to sit with his back to the wall, drawing a blanket over her, and let her doze.

Sometime later, he heard the chime of the watch. He hadn't fallen asleep - the potion wouldn't let him - and he'd started at noises in the house that seemed to be nothing. Ferry stirred at that, and then shook her head, and said "Potion?"

He reached across her and handed her the other vial, then a "May I help you dress, m'lady?"

That made her laugh, and they made short work of getting themselves ready, putting on shoes and stockings, making the bed up. She took the sheet down to where the laundry went, and came back, murmuring. "Just barely daylight out there. We should get going, you said?" as he was finishing upstairs.

He nodded and handed her the scarf. "I don't suppose there's a map here?"

Ferry thought for a minute, and then nodded, leading him back downstairs, to a little room with books, and pulled out a book of maps of the Forest. Rufus traced his fingers over the page.

"We're here. My cottage is here. We want to circle down here, then up. About five miles."

"Wouldn't it be shorter to go straight across?"

"It's wide open. Very easy for people to spot us. And there's bogs, here and here. Man with some nasty dogs, here. And there's farms here and here, where people might be out in the morning, spot us."

Ferry frowned. "Right. The long way round it is. What's the best route?"

Rufus showed her, in more detail. "If we get separated, I want you to promise you'll go. Go to Ytene, go to the village,

go to Boar Court, whatever's closest. Just get yourself away.
You won't be able to help me by staying."

He could see she wanted to argue, and he cupped her
cheek. "I can't fight if I'm worried about you. And people
will listen to you, won't listen to me. We should use that if
we need it."

Another face, but she couldn't argue with that. And
didn't. "Sensible woman," he murmured. "Got the route?"

She traced it out with her fingers again, asked a question
or two about landmarks, and then nodded.

It was a long trek through uneven ground, keeping to
the woods where they'd be much harder to spot. It was
still chilly in the morning, but enough that most people
weren't out and about until they were an hour in, and
well into the woods past Fritham. Once they had a quiet
copse of trees, he paused to give Ferry a rest, and then a
"We'll need to go careful. If Star's in the meadow she
likes best, she'll be just east of the house, tucked into the
woods. Good grass. There's bog to the northwest of there,
going back to the road, but if you go straight north, it's
fine."

A thought occurred to him. "Do you know which way is
which?"

She glanced up, then made a rough calculation. "Did all
right in astronomy, fortunately. That way, yes?" He considered, then nodded. "Slightly off. You'd have learned further
north, yes. Adjust by... about this much." He showed her
with his hands. "But close enough. I hope."

Ferry shook her head at that and then took a moment to
repin her hair. "You're expecting trouble," she said finally.

He nodded. "I - this is too easy. I hope I'm wrong, but
there's. I can feel something off. The birds, I don't even
know. Get to the main road if you're running. If you're

already spotted, maybe the road will have someone who can help, and at least it'll be a clear run."

Ferry let out a long breath. "I hope I don't have to." And then a "We should get on."

Rufus helped her to her feet, and they set out for the last leg of the trip. It wasn't until they were almost to the meadow that he heard something wrong. Voices, where there shouldn't be. Close to his cottage.

He held his hand out, gesturing to her to be silent, then they cautiously made their way forward. The meadow had several mares in it - including Star, still wearing the pack harness she'd worn the night before. The halter lead was still looped through one side of the pack. He let out a breath, a bit louder than he meant, and he heard something behind him startle.

A small cluster of deer burst out behind him, and he could hear the voices of men, raised now. "Shut your mouth, it's a bloody deer."

Rufus leaned close to her. "We get you on Star, then we see if I can get one for me." Ferry looked like she wanted to argue, but after a moment she just nodded.

From the edge of the clearing, Rufus tried to figure out how to get Star's attention. He didn't want to whistle or call, and finally he held out his hand flat. He had nothing for her, but a moment later, Ferry put a sugar cube in his palm.

He was startled, and she shrugged her shoulders and murmured "From the folly. I thought we might need a lure." Before either of them were tempted to say more, Star made her way over, with a soft noise, whuffling at his hand and delicately mouthing at the sugar cube. Rufus settled his hand on her halter, adding another lead, tying them up, and then gathering another lead and halter from the packs she still carried.

It wasn't quite a saddle, but there was enough space with the packs to give Ferry something to help her balance. With two leads, she'd have a better time steering.

One of the other mares came, a deep bay his mother had named Lace. He got the halter on her, and was easing onto her back when he heard the voices, louder, and then a sharp "Oy!"

THIRTY

THE NEW FOREST

Ferry was away before she even thought it. She felt Star's hindquarters bunch, and it was all she could do to twist fingers into the mare's mane and hold on as best she could. It was terribly hard, without stirrups. Her skirts caught on branches and the forest undergrowth and threatened to pull her down.

It was a near thing, several times, the mare's hooves sliding more than once on the uneven muddy ground, Ferry holding and trying to balance. She heard Rufus shout something, couldn't make sense of it, but Star put on an extra burst of speed like some large predator was chasing.

She heard the shouts behind her, but the mare was well through the grove of trees, back toward the road. She thought. She hoped. It wasn't until they were cresting up on the road that she could rein the mare in, using her seat as best she could to bring the mare down to an uneasy walk for a minute. It took her several tries before she could get the mare to settle, without bouncing back into a jangling trot and wanting to be away.

"There, Star, let's see..."

Then she saw and didn't want to.

A burst of light, back where she'd left Rufus, something golden and bright and complicated. Not a natural light, not even something like the sun. It looked like those paintings of angels appearing, all sharp angles and hard lines and utterly unreal. Then it edged with a sickly green, and she had to stop herself from crying out.

It felt like everything stopped for a moment, like it shattered.

She heard a clatter of sound, too nearby, and that was enough to get her to look wildly around, realise where she was. She was on the road, if she kept going, took the right, she'd come to Ytene.

"Miss, are you..." She heard voices behind her, but not the words, she lost them, as she let the mare have her head. Faster. Fastest. She didn't have time to think, didn't want to think, about whether there was any help for Rufus, she only knew she had to get to Ytene.

Someone had to.

The mare was uneasy, she could feel it. Ferry could only hope the road stayed even enough. No stones. No holes. She was holding so tightly to the bare essentials of what she needed to do that they almost went past the turn. There was a stomach-clenching moment when she could feel herself start falling, sliding, as she shifted to try to get the mare turning. Then somehow, miraculously, Star was under her again, and leaping forward once more.

From there, the road was narrower than she wanted, overgrown with branches. She kept having to duck her head to avoid them, making it hard to see where she was going. She just clung and rode and clung and rode, until she could hear the sound change, of stonework under the mare's unshod feet.

"Hey, what - "

Ferry heard someone call out, but she was trying to get her hair out of her face, and her breath back, and she could barely see. She managed a "Lord Carillon, please."

She was terrified, all of a sudden, enough that she completely lost track of which way was up. She slid down Star's too-smooth side to land in a heap on the stone mostly on her back.

It wasn't a hard fall - not a long way down, it's not like anyone was moving. But it knocked the wind out of her, and the words.

"Stay there, Ferry."

It was a brisk voice, and she had to blink several times to realise it was attached to Carillon. "I - Rufus, I can't."

"You stay right there." He was firm, and she wondered for a moment, in the midst of all the other chaos in her head, if he knew the Words of Command.

She couldn't argue with it. He said something to someone else, who murmured "Come along, love." And a "What's her name, the mare?"

"Star." Carillon said. "Put her in the near stall, check her over quick, thanks." Then he settled down, on the paving stones, by Ferry, and said "You lie there, and tell me. Take a minute to catch your breath if it'll help."

She had to take a moment or two. She couldn't get her head to stop spinning. She could hear a stall door closing, words she couldn't make out. And then she could try to explain.

"Rufus." This time it was carefully measured. "He - they kidnapped us, and we got out, but they've got him, down near his cottage. Oh, that doesn't make any sense."

Carillon made a muffled noise, like he was swallowing the sound, then said, "He's in trouble now?"

Ferry nodded.

Carillon called out "Benton. Get on to the Ministry, pronto. Edgarton should be in. Same matter I asked about yesterday. Things have come to a head. Will have more for you in a few minutes. Tell him he can come through the portal inside fifteen."

It got a very sharp "Sir." from wherever the man had got to. And then Carillon was leaning forward, very intent. "What do you know, Ferry? Take it piece by piece."

She'd had enough of a chance to catch her breath, this time was easier. "Last night. After you left. They took us. Drugged me. Think they hit Rufus on the head. Tied us up in a tithe barn, the one near..." She struggled to remember the name. "Landford."

"There we go, that's what I need." Carillon's voice was calm, reassuring, and something in her wanted that praise, solidifying the bog she was floundering through.

"We got out - climbed up, I made a light, it was gorgeous." She was babbling, and she knew it, but she was swept away by the beauty of it in her memory. "And we got a rope and climbed down. They'd left a man and a dog, we think, the other side. And walked and walked and my feet hurt, and then we walked in a stream, and it was cold, and we got to the folly at Boar Court. Nice and safe. And we..."

She stopped talking abruptly, and blushed a deep red, she could feel heat rising.

"Needn't go into that." It was very matter of fact, with none of his usual feigned innocence or even his teasing. "Not my place to pry, unless you need help with a thing."

She shook her head. "It wasn't like that, sir." She gathered herself, then a "We stayed there until dawn, cut across country. Trying to get to you, to tell you, but we had to - avoid the towns. Too much risk they'd see. Stop us. We got to the meadow near his cottage, got Star, Rufus got me up on her. He was putting a halter on another of the ponies, and then they saw us. Men. I got free, but I looked back and there was this light, all sharp and it hurt my eyes, and it made me ache. And scared."

The last part came out in a long rush, and at the end, she wanted to look away and hide. Something in the telling had opened her up and laid her bare. "He needs help. Please. Please help."

Carillon nodded, and then he was rolling up onto his feet, with a "Can you stand, then? Let's get you inside somewhere, and a drink, while we sort out the next bit. Benton's gone to get things in motion. Star's in the stall there, see? All safe. But we'll need your help, I'm thinking, to figure out where Rufus is."

Ferry swallowed and said "I. I will. Of course."

Carillon nodded and helped her to her feet, a strong arm holding her up. Then he was guiding her into the back of the massive house, into a warm kitchen, then down a long hall into a formal entry. She barely glimpsed a man was arguing with the mirror on the wall.

THIRTY-ONE

THE NEW FOREST

Rufus was halfway onto Lace's back before she bucked at the noise. He got a leg over as they started shouting. "You. There. Stop."

The mare stepped back, clearly afraid, and before he could get a word out to try to calm her, she bucked again and pivoted. Rufus went tumbling to the ground, barely getting his hands up over his head as she went charging off. He pushed himself upright to find three men - Will and two others - advancing on him.

He fumbled for anything that might help him fend them off, grabbing a large stick. Not much use against the knives two of them had, but something, maybe.

"Johnny thought you'd be coming back. Couldn't stay away." That was Will. "Set us here."

One of the other men was creeping up to one side, and Rufus swung the stick, giving himself enough space to get to his knees, work on standing.

"Sneaky, you getting out of the barn. Johnny took it out on Douglas. Pity. Liked Douglas."

It was casual, the acceptance of the violence, and it took

Rufus a moment to register the past tense. Something in it must have shown.

"Nice sum for his wife, there'll be. Johnny doesn't take it out on the family. Not without good cause. Now, your little bit, that's cause."

Rufus swung again, trying to keep them back, venturing a glance behind him, trying to figure out exactly where they were. He could see bracken behind him, and then a bit of clearer ground, off to the left. There was bog under there, somewhere, but he wasn't sure of the edges with the ground warming and shifting.

"You're the ones kidnapped her. Woman's got a right to escape."

This got a tsk from one of the men, ferret-faced and tall. "Women should do what they're told. Stay where they're put."

Rufus kept backing up, food by foot, careful and steady. "Funny how that didn't work out for you." He was trying for bravado, and it came out wrong.

Will advanced, with a growl. "Don't you speak against Johnny. He gave you a chance."

"Gave me a chance? Set me up. Threatened me. Before I'd thought of going against him, mind."

"Bought you beer."

"My price is a lot more than a couple of pints, Will." That sounded a little better. Another step back, feeling the rise before the land dropped again. "What are you supposed to do to me then?"

"Kill you. No one'll look for you."

"Ferry will."

"Oh, we've plans for her, too."

Rufus could only hope they hadn't remembered that Ytene was as close as it was. A mile and a bit. Not so far if

Ferry kept on Star's back. Maybe they'd forgotten there was someone there again, or they hadn't noticed Carillon taking an interest in them. All three, preferably.

"Oh?"

"Not telling you. But she goes near the village, well. The village won't be seeing her."

Rufus kept climbing, swung at the ferret man again, and then sucked in his breath. "Well."

Master Burleigh had told him, once, about protection magics. The great magics. How you could pull all the energy into you and send it out. That it would do nasty things, unbalanced. Or it could be like a hedgehog, all over spikes.

It was dangerous. Master Burleigh had been so clear about that. Could send men out of their heads.

But it was the thing he might do that they wouldn't expect before he did the thing they did. So he held his breath for a moment, building up the ball of heat and fire in his belly that he'd learned so long ago. Then he pushed it out, throwing his arms up in the air. Good thing he'd not let all the building magic free before, that it was still there, bursting at the seams.

And then he pivoted, and turned to run, as fast as he could. Up over the ridge, down the other side, dodging the stump of the tree that had come down when he was five. Down to the edge where he'd been forbidden to play.

He could feel the ground begin to give as he ran on. He pulled as hard as he could, calling that energy back into him, down, to make little islands under his feet as they touched the surface of the bog, just enough to hold him.

He hadn't done it for years. Not since Master Burleigh went, not since magic was all about pain and loss and not being good enough, not a thing you did with joy. He made it halfway across the bog, reached a hillock of sturdy ground.

The three men were just at the edge of where the bog started, and he reached out, with his mind, to solidify the area nearest them, just enough. So it would be sodden. Not solid ground, but not treacherous. Enough to make them think it was safe.

Now, he just had to hope they didn't have pistols, or throwing knives, or something of the kind.

Part of him - a very distant part at the moment - hated what he was about to do, but it was the only thing he could think of. There were horrible things going on that these men had chosen. Not just chosen, but kept choosing. And Ferry might need help. The twilight nightjars certainly did.

So Rufus stood, and he waited, and waited, as the men walked and swore and cursed at him. He waited until they were just about between the edge and where he stood.

"Don't you remember why Johnny wanted me? I never forgot." He took a deep breath. "I went to war. I came back. You forgot that too."

He let the magic flow away, flooding back out into the bog, and he saw the three of them sink, immediately, past their waists. "Don't struggle," Rufus called out. "If you don't fight, you might still be alive when I get back."

They were far enough apart not to be able to help each other - not that there was much help, without someone with a rope and something solid to pull against. He inhaled again, firming up a narrow path that skirted widely around them, back toward the meadow.

THIRTY-TWO

YTENE

There was a flurry of activity that Ferry couldn't begin to make sense of. An intense discussion with someone through the mirror, and Carillon gesturing at the other man, who went off somewhere else.

She sat down, heavily, in a chair in the hall, rubbing her hands, until there was a break when someone might tell her what was going on. It took a couple of minutes, then Carillon was back, bending over.

"Ferry, we have a rough plan. Edgarton's sending a few of the Guard through to help clean things up. A small party immediately. We have a portal here, have had one for centuries."

She blinked. She'd been through portals, of course, but they were rare in private homes. Incredibly expensive to build, and an ongoing problem to maintain. "Portal?" she asked.

He nodded. "Edgarton's senior at the Ministry, responsible for matters like this. He'll want to talk to you, eventually. Now, when his picked staff come through, can you ride with us, to where you were?"

She closed her eyes, thought about it, and said "Most of it. I think. I know about where the cottage is. Rufus showed me on the map, this morning. I can show you. Whoever."

"There's a clever woman." Carillon had that approving tone in his voice again, and a part of her leapt at the praise. "Can we put you on a horse again? Or do you need to ride behind someone?"

Ferry took a breath. "Don't suppose you have a saddle would suit Star?"

"Likely we do. Let me go to see to that, while Benton's managing the portal. Benton's my valet. Been with me a decade. Invalided out after Mons." He was reaching for her hand as he spoke. "Come along. We'll want you mounted up. You all right with the skirts? We don't really have time to hunt up breeches that might fit, but I think we have a sidesaddle somewhere."

"I'll manage." And then shyly, a "Sir."

"My responsibility to sort this out. Only..." He stopped suddenly and said "Never mind. No time for that now." Carillon ushered her back out to the barn and left her to reassure Star and feed her another sugar lump, coming back with a proper bridle and sidesaddle that fit well enough. Ferry led her out into the courtyard and stood there, entirely uncertain what to do while Carillon went to saddle his own horse.

Carillon had just joined her, leading a tall and rangy black mare with bright white socks and a blaze, when there was a sound like a harp string breaking, and then the clatter of hooves. Three horses, four, six, with riders in sharply tailored coats, the deep blue coats of the Guard. Four men, but - two women. Which made her blink. One of them rode forward, deep auburn curls peeping out from under a wool cap that covered most of her hair.

"Be welcome to Ytene, and my demesne." They were the ritual words, the things that would let them be here, not raise the protections against those who went armed.

One of the women saluted, promptly. "Edgerton's respects, sir. He said you had someone who could show us where to go."

"Ferry Wright, here. Up you get, Ferry. We're hoping to find a young man, ginger hair, about Ferry's age, but - three men, you said?" Ferry nodded. "We're chasing him, and we don't know if there are others around. About a mile and a half, road then woods. There are bogs. More after that, but that's the immediate concern."

The woman nodded, and called out a series of instructions in some language that Ferry couldn't understand, then she felt their attention settle on her. "Ma'am." It wasn't the right form of address.

"I'm Captain Lefton. You show us where to go, and then let us do our job. You'll ride up with me most of the way there. When we get close, or if you hear any sign of trouble, you get in the middle of the formation or ride as fast as you can back here. Can you do that?"

"Yes, ma'am. Captain." Ferry wanted to please her, and after a moment, her eyes flicked to the large circular brooch the woman wore and recognised as a Pleasing Token. They were expensive, rare, and exceedingly manipulative.

Lefton laughed and said "I'm not exerting myself. But it does make stubbornly vicious men stop in their tracks when that's needed."

Ferry nodded, and the captain lifted her hand, the others falling into a precise V shape behind her. Lefton gestured for Ferry to ride beside her, with Carillon in the centre of the row behind. They took off at a brisk trot, which Ferry could manage with the stirrups. Star seemed uneasy, but not too tired for this at all.

The group made it down the road, to where Ferry said "About here's the turn, the cottage is half a mile, maybe? The field we were in is a little to the east."

The captain surveyed the land, and silently gestured two of the men to circle around, then said "Behind me now, next to Lord Carillon. You let me know if you spot anything, but keep quiet as you can."

The next half mile was nervewracking. They were coming at it from a different angle, and Ferry could see, as they rode up, a figure, sitting, watching the scrubland beyond. He startled, when he heard the horses behind him, then stood, then toppled over.

"That's Rufus!" Ferry forgot to keep quiet, but the captain just said, "Let us take a proper look, ma'am."

One of the others rode up closer as if guarding, and the captain called out "Are you in immediate danger, sir?"

"No. Um. No, ma'am? There are men out in the bog. Not drowned yet. They wanted to - they said they were going to kill me. And..." And then he looked around, and he said "Ferry!" rather loudly.

"Sir, let us help. In the bog?"

"I led them out there. They made it clear they intended to kill me. I know this land. I grew up ... there." He gestured, weakly. "Led them out, held the bog up long enough to get to the middle of it. Let it ... fill in." That got another sharp gesture from the captain, and another rider peeling off.

"And then?"

"I was coming back, turned my ankle, lost my shoe to the bog. Couldn't - manage both. Was trying to figure out what to do."

That got a "Well, then. Seems you've managed nicely. We can be managing these. What else should we know?"

Rufus swallowed. "Please, ma'am. I - can we go back to the cottage? So I can explain? Could someone help me?"

Another gesture or two, and the rider nearest him got down and offered a shoulder. They made an odd procession across the meadow, back to a small and very rundown cottage. Ferry could see the damp and discolour where the roof leaked.

Rufus was settled on a chair, and the man did a quick look over, then a "Pardon, this'll hurt." There was a raw sound, like something moving that shouldn't, and Rufus cried out, then blinked "That's. That's..." He couldn't find words before the man cupped his ankle in his hands and said something. "That'll hold the ankle steady. Wear off in a week or so, won't be able to bend it much 'til then. Help it heal. Right nasty sprain."

"Right." The captain was back on the necessary information. "Tell me what you know."

Rufus explained the whole situation. What Johnny had offered. How he'd threatened later. Where his oath bound him and where it didn't. The kidnapping and escape, which made the captain eye both Rufus and Ferry speculatively. He finished with the long trek back here.

"And where do you think Johnny is? Or whoever else?"

Rufus let out an uneven breath. "Maybe at the tithe barn. Maybe they'll have moved things. I don't know." And then a "Pretty sure I know the route they were going to take. Don't know what they'll do without me. Needed me for the bogs."

Captain Lefton drew out a map drawn on silk, and said, "Show me." Rufus traced the line, indicating True Eyeworth, the barn, the route he thought they'd be taking.

"Do you have anything he's given you?" Rufus shook his head. "No money changed hands. Actually, he was real careful of that, now I think on it."

"Nothing older?"

Another shake of his head, then a pause, and a "Have - something of his son's. Blood. Old blood." And then a "Um. Probably shouldn't climb the loft. Up in the loft, back of the top drawer in the dresser, small green wood box. If you bring it down, sir?"

The other trooper climbed promptly, coming back with a small sanded wood box, and Rufus opened it. "We were friends. His son and I. Did the sort of stupid blood oath people make before they make their proper oaths. Not - real binding? But blood."

That got a delighted crowing from the captain, and a "That's quite fine. Where would his mother be, then? Any siblings?"

"Dead three years ago. And no. He was the only one of theirs lived to adulthood."

This got another flurry of orders, and a "We'll be taking it from here. Lord Carillon, if you could bring them back to Ytene, and see to their comfort, Lord Edgarton would be obliged, and we'll be cleaning up this mess and bringing people in for trial if we can use the portal."

"Trial's fine. I'd rather not draw attention to the portal." Carillon's voice was clipped.

That got a wave of the hand. "Initial assay in your court-yard, dose them, take them through unconscious at our leisure, then. Easy."

That made Carillon laugh and relax. "You always were efficient, Lefton. We'll be there, waiting."

Between them, they got Rufus up on Carillon's mare, and walked back through the woods, leading Star by hand.

THIRTY-THREE

YTENE

One rider escorted them back, and they found the courtyard significantly busier than when they'd left. Another two riders had come through, and a man wearing flowing robes in a deep grey wool was just dismounting.

"Carillon, there you are. And these your young friends?"

"Edgarton. Ferry Wright - yes, that family. And Rufus Pride. They've been very helpful. Your Captain Lefton is off tracking down the individuals involved in the plot."

The Guard who'd come back with them saluted, and then there was a flurry of language, fluid and trilling.

Carillon leaned over and murmured "One of the Lost Tongues. Or rather misplaced. Only used within the Guard these days, and they let no one else learn it. Does wonders for coordination."

Ferry made a small noise, and Rufus ventured to settle an arm around her. "You all right?" he asked. The others around them ignored them, and moved off a bit, to make further plans.

"Feel like I've fallen in a well of deep magic. The things most people don't talk about. Know about."

Rufus had to laugh, which made his rib hurt. "You have? Ferry, love, look at me and all the things I've learned and done and seen." And then he shivered, and Ferry looked up at him, tsking.

"You need a cloak or a blanket or something. And some hot tea." She took a deep breath, and then called out "Lord Carillon, I saw your kitchen earlier. Can I make a pot of tea? And maybe a sandwich? It's been a long time since we had a decent meal."

Carillon made a face, and a "Oh, my, yes. There's a housekeeper should be in there, Mrs Mudthon. Tell her to feed you. She'll be delighted."

Ferry offered her shoulder, and Rufus had to make use of it to get going, though once he was walking it was awkward and ungainly, but manageable.

The kitchen itself turned out to be warm, and full of a bustling older witch, maybe in her fifties, who was in the midst of making up packs of sandwiches. She immediately poured them tea, offered to make soup, and pushed sandwiches in front of them to start, then tutted over the bits of the story as they explained why they were so hungry.

It was perhaps an hour later when Carillon came in, and they were finishing up their meal.

"Ah, there we go. Knew she'd see to you. This is why I've not hired from the village, Ferry. Rufus." His eyes were gleaming. "Had to lure Mrs Mudthon here before we could hire others. She's particular about her staff and how things run, but the results are well worth it."

"Go on, sir." The housekeeper was amused.

"She was the housekeeper for my parents. Got hired

away when they died, but as soon as I knew I was coming back...." Carillon reached out to snatch one biscuit, then said "Business. I gather they've got some of the smugglers, but they're still looking to catch Johnny and two others. You'll be glad to know, I suspect, that Will and his cronies didn't come to lasting harm. You must make a statement in court, but I'm confident it'll come out on your side."

He paused, and then asked, "Did you know about a man named Douglas being dead?"

Rufus nodded. "They told me, sir. That I'd end up like him." He glanced at Ferry and said "That's the man with the dog. They said Johnny'd take care of his widow, give her money, but he wouldn't treat you like that."

Ferry shivered, and Mrs Mudthon patted her on the shoulder. "Nice and safe here, love."

Carillon nodded. "And the riders out that direction have taken word to Boar Court. Made it clear you're assisting in official inquiries, you were absent due to the same reason last night, and that neither should be held against you or your work."

Ferry let out a long "Oh" and shivered again, and got another mug of tea set in front of her. "You drink that. Been a long day for you."

Rufus swallowed, and asked, "What do we do now, sir?"

"They'll be rounding people up, bringing them back here. It will be a soc and sac, that's one of the forms of legal court, one we can do outside a formal courtroom. There are some fussy magical pieces that make sure they do properly everything." He reached out for another biscuit and got tutted at by Mrs Mudthon.

"You'll be asked to identify those you recognise - I'll do the same, the ones I saw at the pub, and have seen at other times. Those will be under Words of Truth, so they will stand in court. You'll tell your story. Ferry will. Separately. You'll be asked if you compared stories or not. Answer truthfully and you'll be fine. On that front, this is a straight-forward case."

"And the birds, sir?"

"They've got to find them first. No help for the orchids, though they can go to the Ministry stores rather than smuggled out for cash. The birds we might yet save if we can get them. Whatever else they were carting across. What they're hoping is to get the ship and the crew that would have taken the cargo elsewhere."

Carillon ran his hands through his hair. "I gather there's been a lot of smuggling. No one minds some of it - well, people mind, but it's understandable. Not much money here, hard to get ahead. If they were shipping rum and tea and such, we'd fine the ones we caught, charge the ones who did violence. But we - the Ministry - people in charge - expect a certain amount of this kind of thing. Trying to stamp it out entirely doesn't work. But this is a whole other thing."

Rufus ventured "The violence, sir?"

"That, yes. Killing people is not a thing we can toler-ate. Especially not having lost so many, between the War and the flu. Every person we lose now is - they've done studies, the impact for decades down the line. Above and beyond their families, their apprentices, the people they work for."

Ferry made a noise, like she was thinking about it, then said "That makes sense, sir. You - you'll tell us what we need to do? What the proper forms are."

Carillon laughed, and said "I'll take you both formally under my protection, how's that? You've more than earned it. If you're fed, thought you might want to come have a look at Star, Rufus, we've got her settled in a stall. Nice little mare, did you train her yourself?"

That put Rufus entirely at ease, and he took Ferry's hand as they went out to the courtyard, before the chaos started up again.

THIRTY-FOUR

YTENE

"Are you sure you're not hurt?" Once they'd seen to Star, they'd come back inside, and Mrs Mudthon had tucked them into a room on the ground floor in the staff wing.

Ferry shook her head. "Tired, and my feet hurt. Well. Lot of me hurts. Aches. But nothing bad, not like your ankle. Do, do put it up, please?"

It was the tone of her voice that convinced him. She helped take his good shoe off and then took off both of hers. They settled together, a bit awkwardly on a bed not really designed for two. She took a breath and shifted, settling with her head in his lap, moving until she could look up at him. "There. Much better."

She sounded somehow utterly secure, and he blinked down at her, not sure what to do with her, with this, with anything. Too much had changed, and far too fast.

He set a hand on her arm, not wanting to be too forward before he said. "I don't even know where to start."

She considered, then reached to pull his hand to her

lips, kiss it, and set it on her other shoulder. "What are you worried about?"

What wasn't he worried about, was more the question.

"What do we do now?"

She tapped his hand. "We stay here until they're ready for us, and then we do what we need to in the trial."

"And after that?"

She shrugged. "We'll sort it out. We sorted out getting out of the tithe barn, and we sorted out staying alive. I'm sure the rest of the week will be less complicated."

He snorted at that, he couldn't avoid it. "Aren't you worried?"

"Not so much anymore?" And then she said "I mean, unless you're having second thoughts. About me, I mean."

He was about to pet her shoulder, and his hand stopped. "I'm not. Only. It can't work."

Her voice got a bit sharper. "Why not?"

Rufus tried to explain. "Your family. They want you to marry, money and... the right sort of person. And you've seen now. How awful the cottage is, and the leak in the roof and the thatch coming down."

Ferry took a breath, then said, "I've learned a fair bit about things this week."

It wasn't what he'd expected, at all. "Like what?"

Her eyes closed, he thought because she was concentrating, rather than because she didn't want to look at him. "Needing things." And then she blushed. It was charming, even while he worried about what it meant.

He stroked her shoulder with his thumb while he tried to find words. "Tell me what you mean, can you?"

"In the barn, when I made the light. I really needed it to work. We needed it to work." Her voice turned shy as she said 'we'.

"G'on?"

"I don't think I've ever really needed anything like that before. That's one of the troubles when you have a... the kind of life I've had. With everyone deciding for you, and protecting you, and putting you somewhere like a wind-up toy and letting you go."

The image made him chuckle, before he said, "And you don't like that, do you."

"You don't do that to me. You tell me things, and you let me decide things, and you want me to join in doing things."

"And you like that." It wasn't quite a question.

"I love that. It made me feel - like I could do anything. Giddy. Like the mirabiles."

"Is that why you asked me to bed?"

"Not just that. But it made me - brave enough to ask. The thing I wanted, needed, even though I've been told it's not a thing nice young women are supposed to want."

He frowned at that. "Your people, pardon, have some very odd ideas about how people should work." He considered and then said more quietly. "I learned about needing really young."

She opened her eyes, maybe at the note in his voice. "Will you tell me a bit?"

"We never had much. Mum used to talk about it when she talked about the runes. About how one of them was need. But the one she talked about more.. the one I remember best." He closed his eyes, all the parts he didn't remember, that no one had explained. "The one I remember best, she called Kenaz. The torch."

"Like my light."

"Like your light. Light in dark times, the thing we need most." He shifted to stroke her hair, finding it soothing under his fingers. "I'm in no position to court you, Ferry. I need to figure that out, and I don't know if I can."

She was quiet for a long time, letting him keep touching her. "I can be patient. I can keep refusing to marry anyone else. If the Bainbridges fire me, well, I can find something else. Aunt Annonia would help. Maybe Lord Carillon or someone he knows."

He grimaced. "And if I can't? The village, they'll be angry."

"You can." She sounded so certain, and he wished he could believe her. "Why would they be angry?"

"Lots of people liked Johnny. Liked his family. Owe the smugglers even if that's not Johnny directly."

"I suspect..." Her voice trailed off. "I suspect a lot of them were afraid, too. Like we were. Maybe those people will be happy he's gone."

Rufus shook his head. "I don't think it's that easy."

"The important things aren't." She was going to be stubborn. He could tell.

"Are you sure you're all right? I mean, we..."

That made her laugh, and a "I want to rest and recover before I do anything energetic. But if you're about to apologise for the bedding I asked for, don't you dare."

The tone of her voice reassured him, rather a lot. "I - all right, look, I was afraid you'd think differently in the morning. People do."

"I," she said, dryly. "Am not people. I am Ferry Wright."

He smiled at that, reaching to touch her cheek, and then he said. "So, Ferry Wright. What do you want to do with yourself? Besides be patient for me, you were very clear about that."

She let her eyes close again, quiet for a minute or so, so much that he wondered if she'd fallen asleep. "They told me in school I was good at the delicate magics. I can't embroider, not and have it be right, but I always wondered about weaving. Or maybe spinning, but weaving seems more interesting? More complicated. More different things going on."

"Don't they have machines for that, sometimes?"

"For cloth, yes. But for magical work? You can do a little with machines, but some of it needs people. Only, I don't know how you learn. Other than apprenticing."

He considered. "Maybe someone would know? Lord Carillon, or someone?" He moved to stretch out, shifting his ankle awkwardly, then his arm more comfortably around her. He was rewarded immediately by her wriggling to be closer to him.

He was half asleep when he heard her say "Need this, too."

THIRTY-FIVE

TRUE EYEWORTH

I
t took more than a week for the rest of the details to get sorted out.

The initial hearing was fast. It startled Ferry at how efficient it all was. One minute they'd been napping in the borrowed room. Ten minutes later they had a mug of tea half-drunk and were being shepherded out to seats in the courtyard.

She'd only seen the formality of a soc and sac, the portable court, a few times, and never for something this serious. There were formal words that laid out the boundaries of the court, patterns of movement to the different directions. She could feel something shimmer into existence, a faint pressure on the skin that made everything feel a little warmer and more closed in.

There were the oaths to the Silence, a long string. Edgarton - Lord Edgarton - made one as justice. Something settled over him, like a fine veil that wasn't quite power and wasn't quite magic, and wasn't quite law, but all of them together. Captain Lefton and her Guards took theirs, which were simpler, and Lord Carillon as the local lord. When

Ferry stood to take her much more limited oath, she could feel the magic slide over her. There was a hint of the prickling of pins, but so lightly it passed in an instant.

The way Johnny cried out, it wasn't so easy for him. Rufus settled an arm around her, tentative at first, and then more securely once she leaned into it. She focused instead on the woman who'd come through, capturing the details for the court record.

After that, it was like a piece of complicated music, done by a full chorus and orchestra. One of the plays her parents had taken her to, in what felt like an entirely different life. Dozens of people had their parts, each one acting in turn or together, depending on their role. Her part, when it came, turned out to be quite simple.

Just stand there and speak the truth.

The Silence wouldn't let her do otherwise. Not that she wanted to. But she looked down and away when they asked for the details of what they'd done overnight. Captain Lefton asked permission to speak, and asked instead "Did you spend the time together, not leaving the folly?" And that she could answer easily. And then the follow-up questions about the timing of when they arrived and when they left. More questions about what they'd used there and what they'd talked about that related to the trial.

It wasn't the end, of course. This was just so they could take the people they'd caught off.

Johnny named the other people involved, once the magics were fully invoked, but the Guard still had to track them down. In the meantime, the Guard bundled the prisoners off into a closed cart, to be taken to Trellech for sentencing.

Lord Carillon bustled her off into a carriage and drove her back to Boar Court, full of non-explanations about what had happened. He had insisted Rufus stay at Ytene for the time being, so he wouldn't be alone if anyone got any idiotic ideas in their head.

She had felt exiled. The staff at Boar Court had fussed, Nanny Ogden had scolded, and the children had refused to let her out of their sight. She had three notes from Rufus, dropped off at odd hours, unexpected. But he'd not been able to meet her, and she'd not been able to get to Ytene, they had kept her so busy.

On Saturday, she convinced everyone to let her go to Market Day, and Rufus was waiting at the end of the drive, smartly dressed with a hat on his head and a long coat against the morning chill. She hesitated for only a moment, then flung her arms around him, wanting to kiss him.

"Easy, love. None too steady on my feet yet." He was grinning, though, when she pulled back. "Brought Star and Lace, so we can ride down. Lord Carillon's helped me sort a saddle out for them both. Brace wore off my ankle yesterday, it's a bit weak yet, but mending well."

She laughed and said "You've thought of everything. I've got things I need to get in the village, but will you escort me, kind sir?" And then the words burbled out of her "You look grand."

"Lord Carillon arranged some things for me."

Walking into the village with him was hard. Neither of them was sure of their welcome. People had liked Johnny, hadn't they? They'd looked like it. They led the horses, left them with the inn stableboy, and walked up to the stalls. Ferry slipped her hand into his, for security.

They were met with a warm welcome that startled them both. People had been friendly enough toward Ferry, but this was different. "There you are, they said you were busy at Boar Court. Good to see you," and inducements to look at this or that.

The way they treated Rufus, though, was even better. Where he'd been left on the outside, the times she'd seen him here, it was something different. It wasn't just the inclusive warmth, it was more like people actually looked at him, seeing him for what he was, not what they'd thought he was.

Ferry murmured. "It's like they're seeing you for the first time. And - letting you decide what to do about that," after they'd gone through half a dozen greetings.

Rufus considered, then asked about the young son of one of the next people they saw, and the grandmother of another. He got an invitation to help on a job hauling wood from an older man. All a bit tentative, but he kept trying.

"Ah, I'd love to be a help, but I'm still recovering. And Lord Carillon's offered me work at Ytene, in his stables. He said he'd be down, looking for other people, now he's got his key staff in place. Good place to work, and the food's brill."

This got a series of murmurs, and Ferry bit her tongue until they were away from the crowd, with a "And you were going to tell me this when?"

Rufus laughed and said "Waiting for the right moment. Benton's his valet. Was doing the horses because someone had to help with them. But Carillon wants someone does just that. Training horses for pavo, even, and managing stable hands, and all. And he said he wants me. Proper salary. And he'll help me learn more to do with my magic, or find people who can, he started that already."

His voice turned shy. "Cottage on the estate, by the grazing land, when it gets fixed up. Much more proper than the other. I could court you proper, now I've prospects. The family cottage, I want to fix it up, but it's not, you deserve so much better."

This got her turning to kiss him again, bold and deliberate. "That's a yes, you," she said. "My parents have thrown six kinds of fits, but Lord Carillon's made them leave me where I am. For now, anyway. Long enough for us to sort ourselves out, yes?"

That got her kissed in turn, and when they finally broke apart, there were cheers from several people nearby, and they both blushed.

"We should tell Pross. She'll be so happy. And I'm sure she's got books about managing stables."

With that, they went off to the bookstore, to tell Pross the full story together over a proper tea.

"It is a lovely old estate." Her mother's voice was cautious.

"Yes, Mother, back to the eleven hundreds." The visit was going better than expected. Though, after three years of silence and being near disowned, there was a lot of scope for better. It turned out even her mother couldn't entirely ignore a new granddaughter.

"I think it's gorgeous. All so green and shady." That was Aunt Annonia, a bit cautious on the uneven stones even with her cane. Ferry dropped back alongside, and smiled at her, and at her partner Julia, who did the materia for the metalwork Aunt Annonia could no longer handle. Ferry smiled at them both, and she was glad Julia had come, the way she always supported Aunt Annonia.

"The cottage is back here, but we go through the court-yard, first." Ferry shifted her daughter a bit more into her arms. She met them at the portal without her husband. She thought a little pause before she introduced them to Rufus was sensible.

When they entered the courtyard, there was Lord

Carillon, beaming, overseeing some painting in the stable yard. "Ladies, do be welcome to Ytene. You must be Ferry's mother, though you look young enough to be her sister. And you, I am sure, are her Aunt Annonia. I've been admiring the jewellery work you do. May I call to discuss a commission at your convenience?"

Predictably, that made her mother simper and oblige. Her aunt beamed, and said, "Of course, Lord Carillon, I'd be delighted. This is Julia Penton, she keeps me entirely together, as well as doing most of the metalwork."

Carillon bowed to her as well, and then said, "We've some flowers for you to take back with you, ladies, the gardens are finally coming back."

"You have rather a lot of horses?" That was Julia, doing her best to be pointed in her gentle way, giving Carillon a chance to speak about Rufus.

Carillon beamed. "Oh, yes, doing very well. We're working on training the first crop of foals to ground work now. Rufus is doing splendidly with that as I was sure he would. He's got a very deft hand with understanding how they think, and what they need." His voice was broad, approving, the kind of tone that made you want to lean in and get some of that for yourself.

"And you're training them for what, precisely?" Her mother's voice was still sharp.

Carillon beamed. "I've some small reputation as a pavo player," he said, easily. "We lost so many horses in the War and so many trainers as well. The ones who don't turn into good pavo mounts, we plan to train up for the villages near here. Riding and carriage, a few of the sturdier ones for carting. Plenty of folk around here can't keep a car, and the bigger roads don't go everywhere they need, anyway."

He then said "I won't keep you from Rufus. The cottage

is quite a cosy little place, though I'm having a larger home for the head of the stables built. You can see it there, now they have a growing family. And you must see Ferry's workshop, of course."

Her aunt tilted her head. "She wrote that you'd built it specially? Quite unusual."

"Ah, well, the loom is rather large, and the spaces we had handy weren't quite suitable. The new workshop is here, close to the stable yard, and we have a housemaid who'll help with the little one when Ferry's ready for that. Her apprenticeship is going swimmingly, now we've found a good match for her skills. I'm looking forward to seeing what she does with the renovation of our tapestries here when she's learned their tricks."

Lord Carillon made it impossible for them to argue with him even though she knew her mother thought weaving beneath the family as a skill. Her aunt's jewellery was acceptable, but only barely.

Ferry took the excuse to lead them along to the cottage. They made the turn that let them get a full view of the whitewashed walls and the fresh thatch, and the deep green paint on the shutters and wood.

Rufus was standing by the outside door, waiting patiently. He was wearing the Homburg Carillon had passed along, no longer at the peak of fashion. It went quite well with his fitted coat and trousers. He looked every bit the competent stable master that he was, and Ferry beamed at him.

When they got close enough, he bowed slightly, offering "Good afternoon, Mrs Wright, Mistress Wright, Mistress Penton. Please, do come in."

"Mother, Aunt Annonia, Julia, this is Rufus. And this is our home."

It was not perfect. Ferry was quite sure things involving her parents would never be perfect. But it was very good. And later this afternoon, when she had taken them back to the portal, she would come back to her husband, their broad bed, and all the amusements they could find together.

IF YOU ENJOYED *Outcrossing* and would like to read more of this series, please sign up for my mailing list to get all the latest news and fun extras. Your reviews (on whatever review site you use) are much appreciated, too!

Rufus makes a brief appearance in *Goblin Fruit*, and Ferry appears briefly in *On The Bias*, both later books in the series.

Read on for more historical details about this book and an excerpt from *Goblin Fruit*.

AUTHOR'S NOTES

In the 1920s in Great Britain, the Mysterious Charms focus on a magical community living and loving alongside the history we know. I have plans to explore more of that history in future books, too!

This series grows out of my joined love for mystery, parallel world fantasy, and romances. (And a particular fondness for Dorothy L. Sayers and other Golden Age of mystery fiction and for rolling around in real-world history.)

You can read the books in any order (each one has a happy ending, with no cliffhangers) but the series does have some overlapping characters. As books are published, my website will let you know which books have more of particular characters or settings.

Many of the details in the book are based on things from our world, so here's a little more if you'd like to read further.

Outcrossing is set in the New Forest in south-east England, and I drew on a number of New Forest traditions when writing it. Six of the seven rights that Rufus and Ferry talk about in chapter 11 have been part of the New Forest for centuries. (**Yewbote** is the one I made up.)

True Eyeworth is a magical village in the Forest, hidden by some of the magics that characters refer to, about how non-magical folk just won't go down that road or notice that thing.

Ytene is a landed estate whose name dates back to the Domesday Book, and as in medieval England, various lords and nobles have magical responsibilities to and for different areas of land.

The traditions of **turning out the mares** and stallions in the Forest are still practiced, much as described in the books. These days you can also find websites that will tell you about the lineage of different New Forest ponies.

Rufus refers to the **Naples Scourge** - one of the other names for the Spanish Flu. That epidemic in 1918 had a terrifying death toll, infecting 500 million people (about a third of the population), and killing 3-6% of people in the world. In English speaking countries, it's often called the Spanish Flu because Spain was neutral in the War and did not have restrictions on publishing the real death counts or spread of the epidemic.

If you'd like to read more about this part of history, *The Great Influenza: The Story of the Deadliest Pandemic in History* by John M. Barry and *Flu: The Story Of The Great Influenza Pandemic of 1918 and the Search for the Virus that Caused It* by Gina Kolata are both good books (the first is more about the history, the second more about the virus itself.)

Rufus briefly mentions something that happened at Mons in chapter 24. The actual story of the **Angel of Mons** - a figure or figures of light standing between the

British and German forces - comes out of a fictional story, but it became widely held to be true. Of course, if there were magical forces at play, any number of things might have been glimpsed in the War.

On the fictional side, many of the magical creatures come from my head, but many are inspired either by real animals or by medieval bestiaries or folklore. The ginsies mentioned as being particularly dangerous cause an allergic reaction in people with magic about half the time.

Pavo and **bohort** are based on real medieval training tools and games. Both involve small teams solving magical and practical puzzles (depending on the focus of the game and the challenges set), but pavo is played on horseback and bohort is played on foot. As a result, pavo is the sort of game played by people with money who can maintain a stable of horses with some specialised training and bohort is more accessible to anyone with useful skills. There'll be more about both sports in future books.

If you have questions about anything mentioned in the books, check out my blog or ask me a question through the blog contact form.

www.ingramcontent.com/pod-product-compliance
Lightning Source LLC
Chambersburg PA
CBHW020407180626
46812CB00003B/865